WONDER NO MORE

An Alternate Leyte Gulf

JAMES YOUNG

A SAMURAI ASSUMES COMMAND

IJNS YAMATO
1600 LOCAL
24 OCTOBER 1944

"SIR, what are we going to do?"

Vice Admiral Matome Ugaki took a deep breath.

What do we do indeed? he considered, looking out the flag bridge's shattered windows. He could see a vessel, one of the Center Force's heavy cruisers, smoking profusely and listing hard to port. Without his binoculars and in the deteriorating visual conditions, he could not make out what ship it was for certain.

"Assemble the staff, Lieutenant Commander Ryuunosuke," Ugaki replied. "I will issue my orders once we have a full damage report."

Ugaki could almost feel Vice Admiral Kurita's's presence still, even in the chaos that was the battleship's shattered flag bridge. The stench of explosives permeated the structure, fighting its own battle with the smell of blood, loosed bowels, and still smoldering fires.

Damn the Americans, Ugaki thought. He was still not sure how he'd survived the direct hit. One moment he'd been struggling against the *Yamato*'s heeling over from a sharp turn. The next, he'd been on the deck, gasping for breath amid his comrade's screams. He looked down at the sword clutched tightly in his hands.

Once again, it appears that you and I have survived, he thought, glancing over at the sheet-covered body arranged in a neat row with several others. *While yet again, my admiral is dead.*

For one moment Ugaki's mind turned to another disastrous afternoon, off the coast of Bouganville. He shook his had to clear those thoughts.

This time I am not struggling to escape a sinking bomber, he thought. *No, this time I am in my rightful place.* Turning, he saw that Ryuunosuke still stood beside him.

"Do you need further instructions, Lieutenant Commander?" he asked sharply.

"Sir, Vice Admiral Kurita's orders…"

"I know what Vice Admiral Kurita said," Ugaki said lowly. His grip tightened on the samura sword. The junior officer, after a moment, bowed quickly in acknowledgment. Ugaki watched the man leave the ruined flag bridge.

The Americans have battered us, but if this weather gets much worse we may yet get to our objective, Ugaki thought. *The nation is counting on us. The fleet will not fail.*

It was ten minutes before Lieutenant Commander Ryuunosuke returned, six men following solemnly behind him.

Has this been so terrible that all I have left are junior officers? Ugaki wondered, before quickly recalling the previous two days. He sighed.

First the submarines, now the American carrier aircraft. Perhaps I should thank my lucky stars that we have anything left at all.

"Situation report," Ugaki said. The men all looked at one another, then back at him.

"The *Musashi* is almost certainly lost," one of the men, a lieutenant (j.g.) stated. "She is down by the bow and the water is almost over her forward deck."

"Instruct two of the destroyers to stand by her," Ugaki said. "They'll take off the wounded while the rest of our force comes about."

"*Mutsu*, *Nagato*, and *Kongo* all report bomb damage," a different man, this one a lieutenant, offered. "But thankfully no torpedoes, in part because of *Noshiro*'s bravery in putting herself between a torpedo squadron and *Mutsu*."

Mutsu *is indeed lucky*, Ugaki thought. *First that the fire that started in Hiroshima Bay last year didn't set off her magazines, then that they were able to get her ready for this battle*. What had caused the fire to start in the battleship's magazines was still unknown. Whether sabotage, as some whispered, or the instability of the special anti-aircraft shells she'd been carrying, the blaze had nearly ended the vessel's career in a ball of fire.

It looks like Fate determined her guns were necessary to help save us all.

"Tell Captain Morishita to bring the *Yamato* about," Ugaki said. "Take us back to the west, back into the squall line."

"Hai!" the staff answered in unison, even as they exchanged confused glances.

"We cannot continue to get pummeled by the American carriers," Ugaki explained. "The bad weather is our cloak, at least for the next couple of hours."

"But sir, what of the Southern Group?" Ryuunosuke asked. "If we turn back to the west, won't Vice Admiral Nishimura be their only target?"

Ugaki pinned the man with a hard look. After a

3

moment, Ryuunosuke broke his gaze and looked down at the deck.

"Sorry sir, I did not mean to question you," the junior officer stated quietly.

"Nishimura will have to see to his own devices," Ugaki replied.

Nishimura is a sacrificial lamb, Ugaki thought. *Which is why he is trying to force Surigao Strait with two ancient battleships. I am envious of his opportunity.*

A few moments after Ryuunosuke left, Ugaki felt the *Yamato* begin to heel over in a turn.

Good, good, hopefully this will give us some respite, he thought.

USS GAMBIER BAY
1800 LOCAL

"HALSEY'S BOYS ARE FUCKING CRAZY," LIEUTENANT AARON Mackenzie said as he walked into the *Gambier Bay*'s ready room. "They actually tried to get another raid off in this slop."

"Yeah, well, I'm more concerned about the damn Japs' ability to fly in it," his friend, Lieutenant Mason Murdock, replied. The man was puffing contentedly on a cigarette as he played chess with one of composite squadron (VC) – 10's FM-2 *Wildcat* pilots. The ensign's brow was furrowed as he contemplated Murdock's last move.

Wow Mason, you could have just killed the kid quickly rather than dragging it out, Aaron thought, looking at the board. It was clear to him that Murdock was toying with the more junior pilot.

Guess we all have our ways of dealing with nervous energy.

"Tough luck for the *Princeton*," someone said from the back of the room.

"Better her than us," Murdock replied. "Those yahoos get all the best equipment and get to fly off a huge deck. Meanwhile, I'm sitting here in a glorified merchant ship."

Gambier Bay, as an escort carrier, was under no obligation to try and fly off her paltry air group in the worsening weather outside. Designated as a "CVE" officially, the *Gambier Bay*'s purpose was to provide air support to a landing beachhead until either the Marines or Army could seize an airfield. Unofficially, the diminutive carrier's crew called her a "Kaiser coffin" due to the shipyard that built her and the sheer fragility of her hull. A single bomb or torpedo could, in an instant, kill every man aboard.

Happened to those poor bastards on the **Liscome Bay,** Aaron thought. He'd been aboard the escort carrier *Coral Sea* when their sister ship had caught the tin fish from a Japanese submarine. Several of his friends from flight school had been aboard the doomed vessel. The four men, along with over two thirds of the *Liscome*'s crew, had not survived.

Good ol' **Coral Sea**. *Can't believe she's the* **Anzio** *now.*

"You look like you've seen a ghost, Aaron," Murdock said, moving a chess piece. "Checkmate, Ensign Rhodes."

"Shit," the young officer muttered, clearly annoyed.

"Just thinking about Derek, Connor, and Jim," Aaron said. Murdock grew somber.

"Yeah, it's been a helluva war," Murdock replied, running his hands through his hair. The ensign looked between both men as if expecting an explanation. Seeing he wasn't going to get one, Ensign Rhodes opened his mouth to say something right as the sound of rain on the deck intensified.

"Yep, that tears it," Aaron said. "I don't think we're getting in that last anti-submarine patrol."

"With the way the small boys have been tearing up the

India boats lately, I'm not sure how many of the Japs are left," Murdock replied, stubbing out his cigarette. "You hear about that destroyer escort that sank six of them all by herself a few months back?"

"Yeah, the *England*," Aaron said. "Meanwhile, we haven't even sighted a Japanese ship, even a small one, in months."

The *Gambier Bay* was part of Task Unit 77.4.3, a subunit of Vice Admiral Kinkaid's Seventh Fleet. With six escort carriers and a handful of escorts, "Taffy 3" was perhaps as powerful as a single one of Third Fleet's larger vessels...if one squinted really hard.

"Keep talking like that and you're going to get transferred over to Halsey's carriers as a replacement pilot," Murdock said. "You're going to wish you were back here in a jiffy when you're having to drop a fish on some carrier."

That'd be a lot more funny if I were Rhodes or another **Wildcat** *pilot*, Aaron thought. The FM-2s, while faster than their predecessors, were far too obsolescent to even be considered for using on Halsey's fast carriers. His *Avenger*, on the other hand, was almost exactly the same model flown off the larger *Essex* and *Independece*-class vessels.

"Not that there will be anything left when you get there from what the radio shack eavesdropped on," Murdock continued.

Aaron briefly looked around the ready room, drawing a short laugh from Murdock.

"What, worried someone here might be a Japanese spy?"

No, but one of us might get shot down tomorrow or the next day over land, Aaron thought, then paused. *Okay, fine, that's ridiculous. Pretty sure the Japanese know how much damage they suffered.*

"Insane how long this war's been going on," Murdock

said after a moment. "I wonder if those yellow fuckers are regretting Pearl Harbor now."

Aaron shrugged.

"If so, probably just until the sharks show up," he replied. "Hope they don't give the fish indigestion."

"I hope they don't give those fish a hankering to try international cuisine," Murdock said.

Aaron saw Rhodes look at both of them nervously.

"Don't worry Rhodes, we haven't had anyone go into the drink for at least three weeks," Aaron pointed out. "The mechanics are good, especially with those *Wildcats*."

Murdock laughed.

"Besides, just think about what a sympathetic pick up line that will be when you get back home," the man said, then struck a mock, solemn pose. "'My dear, I'll have you know that I fought off savages, sharks, and simians for this country. Now let me buy you a drink.'"

Rhodes looked puzzled for a second.

"Simians?" the younger man asked, puzzled.

"What is the school system coming to?" Murdock asked, feigning shock.

"Apes," Aaron said. "Lieutenant Murdock regularly compares our opponents to apes."

Murdock shrugged, clearly unapologetic.

"It might be my good Louisiana upbringing," he stated. "Or it might just be I'm pissed off being here in the middle of the Pacific while my parents are back home living out their golden years without me nearby to help."

"You know, there's six of you kids," Aaron replied, shaking his head. "I'm sure they've got plenty of help from the younger ones."

"Dewayne just shipped off for Europe about a month ago," Murdock said, referring to his younger brother. "Got mail the last time you all did as well. Kinda glad he's going someplace civilized rather than these hell holes."

"You have any family Rhodes?" Aaron asked.

"I had two brothers," Rhodes said quietly. "My oldest brother didn't make it back from Italy."

Well, that took a turn, Aaron thought, looking over at Murdock.

"They still sent you out here?" Murdock asked incredulously.

"I wanted to do my part," Rhodes replied defensively.

"No offense, but your poor mother might feel differently," Aaron said. "I mean, I'm glad that my younger brother might just miss this thing."

"If the Japanese had a lick of sense, it'd already be over," Murdock said angrily. "You can look at a map and see that it's past time to throw in the towel for them."

A mess steward poked his head into the room.

"Gentlemen, do any of y'all want some sandwiches?" he asked. "I've got a tray."

"Are they going to serve a meal in the wardroom tonight?" Aaron asked.

"No sir," the steward said. "Captain Vieweg is expecting us to remain at Condition Zebra even if we secure from General Quarters."

Oh for fuck's sake, Aaron thought, sharing a look with Murdoch. *Always a pain in the ass opening, then closing, then opening every. fucking. hatch.* While he could understand the captain's caution given the Japanese Fleet being out in strength, it didn't change the fact it made simple shipboard functions annoyingly difficult.

"I'll grab a sandwich," Aaron said. He grabbed one then, after a second's thought, another half. The steward smiled for a moment at his decision, then immediately became stone faced as Murdock glared at him.

"Something amusing?"

"Yeah, I'm a greedy pig," Aaron responded. Murdock looked about to say something else when he realized Aaron was not about to let him pick at a mess steward for being human.

I don't care how you folks treat him down in the South, Aaron thought. *He's stuck out here just like the fucking rest of us.*

Before the mess steward could say anything else, a familiar form stood in the hatchway behind him. Turning, the mess steward recognized VC-10's commander, Lieutenant Commander E.J. Huxtable, and quickly moved out of the man's way.

"Mackenzie, Rhodes, you've got first ASW patrol in the morning," Huxtable said.

"Aye aye, sir," Aaron responded, looking over at the *Wildcat* ensign. The young man nodded, then stood up from the table.

"I'm going to go get a shower then turn in, sir," he said to Aaron. "Unless you want to go over anything."

"By this point, I think you've flown enough patrols I don't have to babysit you," Aaron said with a wry smile. He could see that Lt. Commander Huxtable was not impressed with his decision, but the senior officer let it slide.

Tomorrow is probably going to be just another boring day in the Pacific, he thought. *While complacency can kill us dead, over preparation just leads to fatigue...which also kills us.*

"In any case, I'm probably not far behind you," Aaron said. "Might as well write the wife."

"Still apologizing for knocking her up again?" Murdock teased.

Aaron glared at him.

"What?" Murdock said, putting up his hands in mock innocence as Rhodes and Huxtable both grinned. "Just thinking maybe we *should* send you over to Third Fleet to see if you're as accurate with a *tor*pecker. War would be over next week."

Aaron started to smile despite himself.

"I swear, Murdock, there's a reason you're still single," he said. "A gentleman. The second half of the sentence is '...and a gentleman.'"

Huxtable was shaking his head as he walked back out of the compartment, Rhodes right behind him. Murdock watched him go, then turned back to Aaron.

"I'm some ROTC filler who would've been lucky to get promoted if war hadn't broken out," Murdock replied. "Maybe if I was from Canoe U like you are, I'd be a little less couth. Simple fact is, I'm going to be unemployed about ten days after this war is over. Which is fine by me, I just want to get back to Baton Rouge in one piece."

Hadn't thought about what I'll do after the war, Aaron thought. *Way too much water between here and Tokyo to start doing that, honestly. Plus it's not like I need any more motivation to get home than Meredith and the kids.*

USS WASHINGTON
0200 LOCAL
25 OCTOBER 1944

"YOU KNOW, IF THOSE IDIOTS ON *NEW JERSEY* FUCK around much longer, we're going to have *South Dakota* three hours astern of us with just a couple of destroyers for a screen," someone muttered the *Washington*'s in darkened flag plot.

Figures it would be **South Dakota** *that had an engineering casualty*, Lieutenant Commander Hank Orrick thought, but he kept a poker face while regarding the coterie of officers standing around the map board. Vice Admiral Willis Lee, currently the USN's most experienced surface combat commander, stood at the head of the table. Of average height and build, with a round face and dark eyes, Lee did not have the same dashing aura as Third Fleet's comman-der, Vice Admiral Halsey. Still, having recently been reas-signed from the *New Jersey* to Lee's staff due to a washing machine incident, Orrick was already preferring Lee's calmness to Halsey's fits of temper. Thinking of the circumstances that had brought him to this point, Orrick had to shake his head once more.

Pretty sure that's the third time it's happened, Orrick thought. *Or maybe just the second, but I'm going to go out on a limb and say this is why men should not try to do laundry.*

"Sir, we can't get anything besides a 'roger' off the *New Jersey*," Commodore Thomas Jeter, Lee's chief of staff, stated from the senior officer's left. An aviator, Jeter was looking at the map with obvious concern as the staff adjusted the position of the Third Fleet ever further north.

"How long did Captain Riggs say he expected repairs to take again?" Vice Admiral Lee asked, rubbing his temples.

How long has he been up? Orrick wondered. *I mean, I know he just caught a couple of hours, but this is getting insane.*

"He's two hours past his estimated time, sir," Jeter replied. "The *South Dakota* can still cruise at twenty-two knots, but he believes that's his current maximum."

"He can't keep running the powerplant at maximum power," Lee observed. "Especially as long as it's been since she's been back to Pearl or the West Coast."

Jeter nodded in agreement.

"Sir, with all due respect, I think we make Third Fleet

staff wake the old man up or live with our decision," Jeter snapped. "We're one hundred miles ahead of the *South Dakota*, and I don't like her being back there by herself."

None of us do, Jeter, Orrick thought. A former aide to Ernest King, Jeter had been the captain of the U.S.S. *Bunker Hill* before being assigned to Lee's staff. To say the two men had not gelled was an understatement.

Lee doesn't feel like he needs an aviator to babysit him as chief of staff, Jeter feels like this is keeping him from commanding a task group, Orrick thought. *Meanwhile, the rest of the staff is just trying to keep us all from getting killed.*

"So what do you propose we do for air cover, Commander Jeter?" Lee asked gently. "Because if your compatriots are to be believed, they've reestablished that battleships without air cover are sitting ducks."

Lee said the last with very little sarcasm, but the fact it was there at all would have been dripping for any other officer. Jeter pressed his lips together and was clearly debating how to respond.

I mean, how many times have aviators claimed to have sunk every Japanese battleship? Orrick thought. *Hell, starting with that Kelly kid back in '41, the Army alone swears they've bagged at least five more **Kongo**s than the Japanese ever built.*

"Sir, Vice Admiral Halsey's staff will have to figure out what they'll do at daylight," Jeter began evenly. "With the *Independence* damaged, no one has done a night search. Like you, I don't have a good feeling about those Japs coming through San Bernadino Strait."

"I'm not in the habit of conducting gross insubordination, Commander," Lee stated.

"Sir, Vice Admiral Halsey was going to form Task Force 34," Jeter said. Orrick could see the man was barely able to contain his frustration. "Then he canceled it. Or *someone* did."

He's not wrong, Orrick thought.

"At a minimum, if we don't turn some of our ships around we'll have the *South Dakota* all by herself in the morning," Jeter continued, his words coming fast. "I think the Royal Navy tried a couple capital ships with only a handful of destroyers right after Pearl Harbor. You know what happened to both of those vessels."

"Who is here from intelligence?" Lee asked.

Everyone shifted around the crowded flag plot.

Fuck, guess that's me, Orrick thought.

"Here, sir," Orrick replied. He pressed towards the map, parting the press of officers.

"What's your best guess on what the Japanese started with versus what they have now?" Lee asked. "Just the heavy ships."

Just thousands of men's lives hanging on my next few words, Orrick thought. *No big deal.*

"Sir, the reports stated there were six battleships," Orrick said. "That's already one more than we were expecting, especially with the crews saying there were *two* of the *Nagato*-class."

"I thought there were always two," Jeter interrupted.

"Yes sir, there were," Orrick said. "But allegedly General MacArthur's boys captured a prisoner who said *Mutsu* blew up at dockside. There are other sources that corroborated this."

Funny thing about breaking someone's codes, he thought. *At times you may get something slightly off.*

"Could she have sank and they refloated her?"

"Could have, yes," Orrick replied. "But how she got here is irrelevant, she's clearly here."

"So two of those new super ships they have with the 16-inch guns, two *Kongo*, two *Nagato*," Lee said. "Two more in the south, but Seventh Fleet is dealing with those."

"Yes, sir," Orrick said.

"And the strike claims they sank three of the ones outside of San Bernandino, which is where the rest of them turned tail?"

"Yes sir," Orrick said.

In for a penny, in for a pound.

"But I personally doubt that the Japanese commander would turn around in these circumstances," Orrick continued in a rush. "This is their last throw of the dice, sir. If we were all that stood between the Japanese and San Francisco, there's not a single one of our commanders that would turn around just because of a little battle damage."

"Does anyone know what Seventh Fleet has in the north?" Lee asked.

There were a few long moments of silence.

"Okay, does anyone know how to get a hold of Seventh Fleet?"

Again, there was silence. Lee shook his head.

"Damn MacArthur and Kinkaid," he muttered. He looked up at the clock.

"Commodore Jeter, issue the following order: We will form Task Force 34.2 in order to support the *South Dakota* and prevent her from getting caught by herself at daylight. Go with the *South Dakota, Washington, Alabama, Massachusetts,* and *Alaska.*"

Well, looks like it's a good thing that "large cruiser" got here a couple months early, Orrick thought. He wasn't quite sure on what had happened, as apparently the *Alaska* wasn't supposed to have arrived for another thirty days. He suspected some chicanery on the part of her captain and crew, but that was well above his pay grade.

Just hope them being green doesn't make this any harder, Orrick thought. *Already going to be a nightmare for those ships detaching from the carriers and forming up in the dark.*"

"Sir, we'll set the rendezvous point once we issue the initial order," Jeter replied. "Do you have any preferences?"

"No," Lee replied. "Just keep us from having any collisions if you could."

"Aye aye, sir," Jeter said. Lee turned to Orrick.

"As far was we know, the Jap carriers only have those two hermaphrodites with them, correct?" Lee inquired, referring to the "battle carriers" *Ise* and *Hyuga*.

"Yes, sir," Orrick replied.

"Well if the *New Jersey* and *Iowa* can't handle the two of them, their captains should be hanged," Lee said simply. "Same cruiser line up as planned. Courtesy copy the *Intrepid*. If anyone is going to break ranks and follow us, it's Rear Admiral Bogan."

Jeter nodded.

I hope the Japanese don't make a fool of me in the morning, Orrick worried. *Oh well, if I'm wrong what are they going to do to me? Send me thousands of miles from my wife?*

"Gentlemen, we had a chance to finish this in June and I talked Vice Admiral Spruance out of it," Lee said, looking around the room. "That's why we trained in September, and I'm confident we'll shoot the shit out of some Jap battleships tomorrow if we have to."

Orrick looked at the map as Lee continued.

"But let's make sure we don't give Seventh Fleet a heart attack when we show up," Lee continued. "I was with Vice Admiral Kinkaid around Guadalcanal. He's an excitable sort, doesn't like surprises. So make sure we send a dispatch plane off at first light."

"Aye aye," Jeter said.

"I'm going to bed," Lee said. "You don't take 'no' for an answer unless it's Vice Admiral Halsey himself. I'm not going to have his damn staff end up with us leaving some baby carriers and destroyers out to dry. We'd never hear the end of it from the damn Army."

That brought a slight chuckle around the room. With a last nod, Lee turned and left the flag plot.

Orrick did some quick math as he measured distance.

We'd be near the escort carriers by around seven tomorrow morning if the **South Dakota** *fixes her boilers soon*, he thought. *Couple hours after dawn. At least it won't be another night fight.*

USS Johnston
0250 Local
24 October 1944

"Jesus, it sounds like someone is getting pounded," Ensign Jack Murphy said, looking up from a letter home to his mother. The young officer was referring to the speaker mounted on the U.S.S. *Johnston*'s radio shack bulkhead. The *Fletcher*-class destroyer was cutting through the waters just off Samar Island, her compartments mostly blacked out to prevent giving away Taffy Three's position.

"Not someone, the damn *Japs* are getting their asses handed to them," his companion, Lieutenant (j.g.) Dennis Schuler stated, voice filled with awe.

Technically, the little destroyer should not have been able to pick up the radio transmissions from far to their south. Furthermore, the two officers were nominally supposed to be standing watch and assisting the officer of the deck, Lieutenant Hagen, *Johnston*'s gunnery officer. However, once the senior officer realized the freak in atmospherics that was allowing them to pick up Vice Admiral Oldendorff's ambush, he'd released both junior officers to listen.

Mom can wait, Jack thought. *She'll forgive me later.*

"Is that the destroyers going in?" Jack asked, barely able to discern the call sign. "Wonder who that is in charge of them. Seems to have a definite hold on things."

"Captain Coward, I imagine," a familiar voice said from behind them. Both officers and the three sailors in the compartment jumped up from their seat as Commander Ernest Evans walked into the radio shack.

"Sit down, sit down," Evans said genially. "I take it you all forgot that I have a speaker piped into my day cabin?"

Jack and Lieutenant (j.g.) Schuler shared a look of pure terror, as did all the sailors.

"No worries," Evans said, yawning. "If we've got a front row seat to a radio drama, might as well see how it plays out."

"Aye aye, sir," Schuler replied. At the point, Lieutenant Hagen poked his head in.

"You guys need to keep it down in…oh. Hello sir, sorry to wake you."

Evans waved him off, focusing intently on the radio. He grinned, and Jack felt a slight sense of disquiet at the look.

The only reason that's not how Crazy Horse probably looked at Custer right before the scalping started is because the Old Man is Cherokee, not Sioux, Jack thought.

"Gentlemen, what you're hearing is a textbook destroyer attack," Evans said. "I imagine our boys are going in with radar and actually just using their torps rather than firing back at that Japanese screen."

With Evans giving them a description, Jack could just imagine things in his head.

Dark as hell out there, with cloud cover to boot, he thought, thinking about the worsening weather.

Evans looked at his watch.

"Now listen to see what you hear in about seven minutes or so," he said, tone almost wistful.

"If the torps work," Hagen said grimly. Evans nodded at that comment.

"We've done a lot to fix the fish," Evans replied, then saw the blank look on the younger officers' faces.

"Beginning of the war we had a lot of duds," he explained. "Everyone did, from the submariners to the aviators. How many torpedoes did you bounce off that Jap battleship during the Friday Night Massacre?"

A pained look crossed Hagen's face even as Jack wondered what the captain was talking about.

"I think the *Aaron Ward* should have hit her at least three times from that range," Hagen replied.

That's right, Lieutenant Hagen was at Guadalcanal, Jack thought to himself. *First Guadalcanal, as I recall.*

"Why didn't the torpedoes work, sir?" Schuler asked.

"We didn't test them prewar," Evans said. "Too expensive. Too bad the man who made that decision went on to become an admiral rather than getting shot for it."

Jack saw the same shocked expression on Schuler's face he was sure was crossing his own.

"Shame the fly boys took care of the other Jap fleet earlier today," Hagen said. "Would have loved another crack at them."

Evans turned from the speaker and smiled.

"Be careful what you wish for, Robert," Evans chided with a smile.

"Sir, I think you're being a bit hypocritical," Hagen replied with a broad grin. "Something about 'I intend to take this ship into harm's way' comes to mind."

Two of the sailors laughed before they could stop themselves. Schuler favored them with a hard look.

I feel like I missed something, Jack thought. *I guess that's what I get for getting aboard as a replacement.*

His predecessor had been "washed overboard" in the middle of the night. No one had seen the man go, and allegedly there'd been a note the captain had ordered burned.

Not sure I'd jump off a ship in the middle of the Pacific over a dame running off with another man, Jack thought. *But that's also one of those decisions you don't get to reconsider, unfortunately.*

"I meant what I said in that speech, gentlemen," Evans said, his tone firm. "If this vessel sighted a Japanese battleship tomorrow, I would only hope we would have an opportunity to…"

The radio was suddenly a cacophony of conversation, the voices distorted by distance and atmospherics. All of the men in the compartment listened intently, but Jack had little clue what was going on until Evans deciphered it for him.

"Sounds like a good spread of fish," he observed. "At least two large vessels blown up, one of them maybe a battleship. Of course, everyone thinks they've sunk a battleship at night."

"You never forget one when you see it up close," Hagen said. "Even worse in daylight though."

"Is it true your last captain tried to duck behind a bulkhead when that *Kongo*-class fired at you the next dawn?" Evans asked, raising an eyebrow.

"Sir, if I could've clicked my heels together and disappeared up my own asshole, I would have done it," Hagen said earnestly. "At least if it happens again I'll hopefully have some guns to shoot back with."

He looks positively haunted, Jack thought. His uncle had once sworn he'd seen Jack's long dead grandmother Christmas Eve night. While Jack was sure that had more to do with the half bottle of whiskey than any maternal after-life visits, Hagen's face bore almost the exact same expression Uncle Hank's had that December morning.

"The battleline just opened up," Schuler remarked. Evans was about to reply when the radio abruptly went dead. The sailors immediately began tending to it, checking wiring.

"Sir, looks like whatever was letting us hear the fight we moved out of," one of them said apologetically after five minutes.

"Well, looks like we go back to being carrier escorts rather than spectators," Evans sighed. "Speaking of which, you'd best get back on the bridge, Robert."

Lieutenant Hagen nodded, heading forward out of the radio shack.

"As for you two, there's no reason for you both to get no sleep," Evans said. "Between Third Fleet and Olden-dorff, I don't think there's a whole lot of ships left to shoot. But we'll probably have to deal with more of those damn planes in the morning."

"Third Fleet didn't have a good time of it yesterday, sir," Schuler said. "Sounds like the Japanese carriers got the *Princeton* and put a couple of bombs into the *Independence*."

Evans shook his head.

"Well there goes that night carrier experiment," he muttered.

"Sir?" Schuler asked.

"Nevermind," Evans said. "Just a conversation I had with one of my classmates when I was last in Pearl."

A runner poked his head into the radio room.

"Sir, Lieutenant Hagen says the visibility is getting worse," the sailor said. "Down to eight thousand yards due to haze."

Evans looked as if he was pondering something for a moment.

"Tell him to make sure to set a good radar watch, but we don't need to wake up any more lookouts," Evans replied. "I suspect Rear Admiral Sprague will have a plan he'll pass along, and we've got plenty of sea room."

"Aye aye, sir," the sailor replied, then was gone.

"Murphy, you finish your letter to your mother then get to bed," Evans said with a smile.

I guess it's true what they say about the captain sees all and know all, Jack thought, feeling his face flush.

"Sir, someone has to do it," Jack said sheepishly. "She claims she never hears from the other three. Something I intend to fix if we ever are in Ulithi at the same time as *Alaska*."

Evans shook his head.

"Not surprised she hasn't heard from your brother if he's on her," Evans noted. "Scuttlebutt is her captain was lucky he didn't 'accidentally fall over the side' as hard as he worked that crew. She's out here six months earlier than expected."

Jesus, Jack thought. *Okay, maybe I'll go easier on Tommy when I see him next.*

"Still, it only takes ten minutes a night," Evans continued. "Just don't get yourself thrown in the brig for beating your brother's ass."

"Yes sir," Jack said, smiling. "I would never strike a superior officer."

Evans shook his head with a smile as he walked out the aft hatch. Hagen watched him go, then turned back to look at Jack.

"I didn't know you were related to Tommy 'Gun' Murphy," Hagen replied. "You don't look anything like him."

That's a long story we just don't talk about in the family, Jack thought, shrugging.

"We get that a lot, sir," he replied.

SPIT ON BOTH HANDS...

USS GAMBIER BAY
0540 LOCAL
25 OCTOBER

AARON STOOD at the *Gambier Bay*'s island as the small carrier's elevator finished raising a replacement FM-2 *Wildcat* to the flight deck. The deck crew immediately began manhandling the dark blue, stubby fighter into position near the stern.

"The captain is fit to be tied," he remarked to Rhodes, gesturing upwards to where the carrier's master could be heard shouting at the CAG.

"Sorry sir," Rhodes said, looking back at the island.

I swear he looks like a man who just ran over his neighbor's puppy, Aaron thought.

"Not your fault your engine took a dump," Aaron said simply, then pitched his voice lower. "Not sure what yelling at the air boss is going to solve either. Other than to make him feel better."

Rhodes cracked a smile. Checking to make sure no one else could overhear him, Aaron continued.

"Remember this when you have your own carrier someday," he said, looking Rhodes in the eye. "Sometimes planes just decide to break."

Two aircraft flew overhead in the pre-dawn gloom, their dark shapes and exhaust flames just discernible against the lightening sky.

"Besides, it's not like we've got an important sector anyway," Aaron noted. "If there's trouble, it's going to be from the north."

Taffy Three's staff had rearranged the search sectors after Aaron had gone to sleep the previous night. Rather than having an ASW sector towards the north, i.e., the side further way from shore, Aaron and Rhodes had been given their sector to Taffy 3's south.

If a submarine passed us overnight, realized its error, and is now deciding to come back north then the destroyers are fucking up, Aaron thought. He was no submarine expert, but he knew that move would only be made by a pretty ballsy commander.

Or a suicidal one, he corrected after a moment. *But then again, these are the Japanese we're talking about.* Suddenly he was less certain that things were going to be boring.

"Just glad we're not on the *Ommaney Bay*," Rhodes remarked as the pair turned and started walking towards his fighter.

"Oh? Why's that?" Aaron asked.

"Scuttlebutt is she got an order last night," Rhodes said. "Initially the radio shack thought it was for us and sent a runner down to wake up the ordnance guys. Something about a dawn search for surface ships."

Aaron turned and looked towards the south where the *Ommaney Bay* and "Taffy 2" were located.

Would've made more sense for them to have us do the north search and Taffy 2 send some anti-submarine patrols between us, Aaron thought. *But I guess who am I to judge a…*

The towering waterspouts that appeared around the U.S.S. *White Plains* were sudden and startling. One moment the *Gambier Bay*'s sister ship was launching her own dawn aircraft, the familiar outline unbroken. The next, four tightly-spaced, odd-colored towers of water appeared between that vessel and where Aaron was standing. The *crump* of explosions could be heard a few moments later.

"What the fuck?" Rhodes asked, standing stunned. Aaron shoved the ensign.

"Get to your plane!" he shouted, looking upwards. "Air attack!"

How the fuck did a Jap get in without getting detected by radar?! He thought, running towards his own *Avenger*. Looking, he saw his turret gunner, Radioman 1c Kevin Morgan, already strapping in as the plane captain started the engine. The big Pratt & Whitney radial began thundering, its din joined shortly by Rhodes' engine. The noise prevented Aaron from hearing the explosions, but he saw two identical flashes appear on the *White Plains*' deck and her island. These were followed almost immediately by brilliant balls of flame as several spotted aircraft erupted in secondary blasts.

Well shit, this morning just got horrible, Aaron thought. He looked over to see his third crewman, Chief Radio Technician 2c Carson Rizzo, buttoning up his flight suit as he clambered into the *Avenger*'s belly.

"Hell of a time for a head call, Rizzo!" Aaron shouted as he jumped into his seat.

"Jesus Christ, look at her burn!" someone screamed. Aaron spared a second to look over and wished he hadn't. The *White Plains*' aft flight deck had become fully involved, with what was probably an *Avenger*'s full bombload detonating violently. It was what he saw in the afterimage of that flash, however, that nearly made him void his own bladder.

That's…that's gunfire on the horizon, he thought. *Coming from the west…how?*

"Sir! Sir! They're waving at us to go!" Morgan said, pointing back towards the bow. Aaron turned, saw the catapult officer signaling furiously, and made one last check of the *Avenger*'s left and right wing tips to make sure everyone was clear. With that, he advance the throttle and signaled he was ready.

Oh fuck, I'm not strapped in, he thought. With lightning speed, he strapped his belt in right before *Gambier Bay*'s catapult kicked the big *Avenger* forward and off the bow. Resisting the urge to immediately wrench the big bomber into a climb, Aaron nearly jumped in his seat as two crimson columns of sea water bracketed their bomber. A slight vibration told him something had hit the Grumman, but a quick check didn't reveal any damage.

THE *WHITE PLAINS'* ASSAILANT WAS THE *YAMATO* HERSELF. Having found the range at 17,000 yards, the massive battleship's gunnery officer stopped walking her 18.1" shells in a ladder. Even as Aaron was buckling in and gaining airspeed while calling for Rhodes to join up, *Yamato* fired her first full salvo at the now blazing *White Plains*.

The second shell hit had shattered the escort carrier's island, while the flames from her planned dawn strike had cleared her secondary control. It was for this reason that the carrier had continued to steam at near full speed into the wind, even as her compatriots' and escorts had begun to react to fire. The lack of evasive maneuvering meant the next tight salvo produced four hits, each the equivalent of a one-ton bomb. Two pierced the forward starboard and port aft portions of the flight deck, carried out of the ship, and detonated close alongside with severe mining effects. The resultant flooding was of little consequence, however, as the other two shells both pierced the *White Plains'* deck, hangar deck, and into the hull to detonate just above and just aft respectively of the main bomb magazine.

In a terrible, searing instant, the *White Plains* erupted in a horrible pyrotechnic display. Debris scythed outwards from her in a horrible circle, with metal cutting down rushing crewmen on her sister ships in the same column. Split through her keel, the carrier's forward half began to capsize even as it jackknifed backwards. Propellers still spinning under the terrible blackened cloud, the stern plowed forward and into the Pacific's depths. In less than ten minutes of shooting, Center Force had drawn first blood.

IJNS Yamato
0605 Local

"The carrier is blowing up!"

Vice Admiral Ugaki was not sure who had uttered the report, but it was largely superfluous. Even at nearly ten miles, the explosion had been quite visible through his binoculars.

I thought for sure they would be waiting for us, shooting from the darkness with that damnable radar of theirs, Ugaki thought. *Then I thought they would be waiting until it was slightly lighter. Then when we had made the turn south. But no, we appear to have caught the Americans well and truly sleeping.*

"Sir, I owe you an apology," Ryuunosuke said, his voice in awe.

Before Ugaki could answer, the *Yamato*'s firing gong rang once more. Ugaki gritted his teeth, fighting the urge to hunch his shoulders in anticipation of the impending broadside. With a mighty roar that shook the flag bridge and blast which rippled his entire body, six of the battleship's 18.1-inch guns spoke.

Taking that bomb hit and having the windows smashed has definitely made this a more difficult place to command from, Ugaki thought to himself. He nodded at Ryuunosuke in acknowledgment, the ringing in his ears taking a moment to clear. Even with cotton covered by muffs to muffle the blast, Ugaki had severe doubts he'd be able to hear by the end of the engagement.

If I am still alive, that is, he thought grimly. *Any moment now the American battleships will double back to save their fleet carriers.*

"No apology necessary," Ugaki said after his ears stopped ringing and he was sure his junior could hear. "It was a gamble to come down the landward side after we turned south from San Bernadino Strait. If the Americans had been waiting, we would have been trapped against Samar."

The firing gong rang out once more. Bringing up his binoculars, Ugaki saw first *Kongo*, then *Mutsu*'s salvoes bracket the same vessel. He waited until *Yamato* once fired again, then turned to one of the staff lieutenants.

"Tell Division 3 to hold their fire," he ordered. "We will save them for the next task force!"

I need to stop gawking like a tourist and start commanding this force. Ugaki away from from the windows and back towards the massive plot in the center of the flag bridge. Approaching the table, he saw a runner hand a slip of paper to the plot lieutenant. The man nodded, smiled, then reached forward to X out a symbol on the board.

"The *Suzuya* reports one of the enemy cruisers is burning and sinking," the man explained.

"The American vessels seem to be less hardy than usual," Ryuunosuke stated. "That is the second cruiser we've sank."

Something nibbled at the back of Ugaki's mind.

"How many of the carriers have we set ablaze?"

"Three, sir," the plot officer replied. "We seem to have caught them while launching!"

The thought hit Ugaki like a thunderbolt.

"This is not Halsey!" he shouted. The officers gathered around the table stopped what they were doing and looked at him.

"Sir?" Ryuunosuke asked quizzically.

"Think you fool!" Ugaki shouted, waving his hands in frustration towards the burning ships on the horizon. "Each of their *Essex*-class carriers are as big as the *Shokaku* or *Hiryu*."

The gathered men were a study in lack of understanding.

"Even at flight quarters, our carriers did not blow up like this at Midway!" Ugaki fumed. "Nor are they so slow we should be closing the range as rapidly as we are!"

Ugaki could see realization was beginning to dawn on the staff.

They are tired, and we have had a horrible journey, he thought, even as elation swelled within him. *But a great victory is possibly at hand!*

"It is the small carriers, the one the Americans place near their transports," Ugaki continued. He was interrupted by *Yamato*'s guns firing again. As the ringing in his ears calmed down, Ugaki continued.

"The plan worked," Ugaki said. "Halsey must have gone north, after the Gargoyle!"

The roar of an aircraft's engine followed by the high-pitched whine of ricochets caused all of the men present to dive to the floor.

All of these anti-aircraft guns and yet they still strafe with impunity, Ugaki thought angrily. Struggling to his feet, he nearly fell to the floor again from *Yamato* heeling over in a turn.

"What are they doing down on the bridge?!" he shouted at the talker.

"The enemy's aircraft are making torpedo runs!"

Ugaki looked out the bridge windows. Glancing at the cloud coverage, he pursed his lips before coming to a swift decision.

"Tell them to press on," he snapped. "We dodge no more torpedoes!"

"Sir?" Ryuunosuke asked, incredulous.

"Time is not on our side!" Ugaki stated.

The man looked at him dumbfounded.

He probably does not remember when Mikawa smashed an American cruiser force off Guadalcanal, Ugaki thought. *If only Mikawa had pressed southward, he could have ended that horrible affair that night. Instead, he let the carriers scare him.*

"We have to press south, to the beaches, before Halsey returns!" Ugaki barked. "These small carriers do not have the necessary strength to harm us. If we get to the transport beaches, we will stop the invasion of the Philippines!"

Once more, Ugaki saw realization dawn among the staff.

Am I truly surrounded by idiots? Or has fatigue made them dumb and slow?

"General zigzag, no radical turns," Ugaki ordered rapidly, his tone urgent. "We head south at all haste. The carriers are of no matter to us."

Another burst of machine gun fire, this time penetrating the flag bridge, seemed to put a lie to Ugaki's words. While no one in the structure was, screams from the lookout stations above indicated some of *Yamato*'s crew had not been so lucky. Even as the cries continued, Ugaki saw his staff beginning to transmit the directions to the rest of the fleet.

"Sir, I think we are being reckless with regards to enemy aircraft," Ryuunosuke stated quietly, eyes cast downward. Ugaki had a brief flash of anger, his hand tightening on the sword at his side. Taking a deep breath, the senior officer released the katana, then extended his hand to place on the junior officer's shoulder.

I doubt that, by this afternoon, any lessons I impart on fleet tactics will matter, Ugaki thought. *But, in any case…*

"When I was captain of the *Yakumo*, we stopped in Malta," Ugaki began.

Yamato jumped in the water once more as he looked at the map.

"I ran into a Royal Navy commander there who was writing a treatise on raiding an enemy amphibious operation," Ugaki continued. "Curious, I asked him for one piece of advice regarding such a situation."

Ryuunosuke raised his gaze to meet Ugaki's.

"What did he say, sir?" the junior officer asked.

"That raiding an amphibious anchorage is much like turning to piracy," Ugaki replied solemnly. "There comes a point where all the planning has to cease and there is only time remaining for action. 'At that time, a man must turn to piracy for guidance, as the moment for rational thought is over. All that remains is to spit on both hands, hoist one's battle flag, and commence to slit throats.'"

With that, Ugaki adjusted the sword at his waist, turned, and walked to look out the flag bridge at the several columns of smoke raising to his force's east.

Turning, he scanned the sea behind *Yamato*, at the rest of his battle line. Raising his glasses, he allowed himself a small smile upon sighting the largest Imperial ensign he'd ever seen streaming from *Nagato*'s foretop.

*While I doubt we will close to boarding range, we **will** smash every ship off that beach.*

Ugaki felt the *Yamato* shift with her course change. A rain squall was cutting visibility between the super battleship and her prey. With one final blast, the main battery engaged a distant target, then fell silent.

Even the gods are telling me to hasten my way south, Ugaki thought. *So be it.*

USS JOHNSTON
0620 LOCAL

"Stop gawking you idiots! There's work to do!"

If Jack had not been in the middle of rushing back towards the *Johnston*'s bridge from engineering, he probably would have probably recognized the snarling chief petty officer's voice. The *St. Lo*'s hulk was just finishing its capsizing as he reached the bridge.

Final salvo from that damn Jap battleship must have got her square in the engine room, Jack thought. *I knew they called them Kaiser Coffins but holy shit.*

"Sir, Engineering reports they'll have the handles open on the chemical smoke generators," Jack said, out of breath. "They were rusted shut."

Commander Evans turned towards him and Jack instinctively stepped backwards.

Jesus Christ he looks enraged, Jack thought. Realizing that he was about to shoot the proverbial messenger, Evans gritted his teeth and turned back to looking towards the west.

That rain is only going to last so long, Jack thought. *I'm shocked the Japs aren't coming right through it.*

"Sir, radar confirms they're heading south, not towards us," the bridge talker said. "They've also increased speed to 28 knots."

We're saved, Jack thought, fighting to hide the exhilaration he felt. *I'm not going to die in the middle of the Philippine Sea.*

"Goddamit, someone learned on that side," Evans muttered. "Wish someone had learned on ours."

"Sir?" Lieutenant (j.g.) Digardi, the officer of the deck, asked.

"You have the conn, Ed," Evans said in response. "Bring her to heading one nine oh, make all speed. Signal the *Heermann* to follow us, the *Raymond* and *Butler* will continue to escort the remaining carriers. We'll have to come back for the survivors later."

"Aye aye, sir," Digardi said, gulping. The other officer briefly locked gazes with Jack as Evans turned to the plot.

This crazy son-of-a-bitch is about to **chase** *some battleships!* Jack thought. As if he could hear his thoughts, Evans looked up at Jack.

"Wondering if the old man has lost his mind, Ensign Murphy?" Evans asked. Jack paused, then squared his shoulders and started to come to attention.

"Son, I'm asking a question, not berating you," Evans said genially as he stared at the map, gazed out the bridge windows, then looked at the map again.

"Sir, I have many questions," Jack hedged.

"You've heard me talk about the Dutch East Indies and how we surprised those bastards across the way," Evans began. "Remember how I said they returned the favor off Guadalcanal at Savo Island?"

"Yes, sir," Jack replied. It had been of Evans' repeated lessons, emphasizing that the *Johnston* must be prepared for combat at all times.

Probably why we were able to dodge the couple of salvoes the Japanese threw our way but the **Hoel** *got hammered*, Jack thought. *As long as I live, I hope I don't see that again.* Their sister ship had been reacting sluggishly to the incoming shells that had riddled Taffy 3's formation. As traumatic as the *White Plains*' destruction had been, seeing the *Hoel* literally disintegrate had been far worse.

Then again, if this madman has his way I might get to live the experience firsthand.

"The part that I glossed over is the Japanese commander, whatever his name was, had our ships dead to rights that night off Savo," Evans continued. "They had sunk almost all the heavies, and if they'd headed into the anchorage it's possible they bag every transport the Pacific Fleet had at that time. If they'd sank the transports, the Marines would have starved within a week, and the Japanese would have held Guadalcanal rather than losing that entire campaign."

Jack noted the entire time that Evans was working plot calculations.

"The transports are mostly gone, but they left all the supplies on that beach when they left," Evans said. "I'm not sure how many supplies the Army moved inland over the last couple of days, but it's not enough that we need to let the Japanese blow them up."

Evans shook his head.

"Lot more Army boys than those Marines, and I don't think there's enough land for them to live off of, even if we did use to own the place."

Jack swallowed.

"Sir, we're one ship," he said, his voice tremulous. He

swallowed, and continued more firmly. "We aren't going to do much against those battleships."

"No, we won't," Evans replied. "But to paraphrase Lieutenant Hagel right before you came back from astern, we'll do *something* if we 'just get the torps off.'"

Jesus, the whole wardroom is insane, Jack thought. Evans looked down at his math, nodded, then looked at the talker near the back of the bridge.

"Hand me the 1MC," he stated, gesturing for the *Johnston*'s ship wide intercom. The talker, hand shaking, handed the device over to Commander Evans. Taking a moment to gather his thoughts, Evans bent his head. Jack could see his lips moving as the man uttered a quick prayer.

I sure hope he's praying for those battleship down at Surigao Strait to find a magic carpet, Jack thought. His heart was in his throat as the short, barrel-chested captain began speaking.

"Men of the *Johnston*, this is your captain speaking," Evans said.

Jack marveled at how steady the man sounded.

"As you may have surmised, the Japanese fleet that surprised us a little over forty-five minutes ago has broken off the action," Evans said. There were a few scattered cheers from outside before Evans continued.

"I believe the enemy is taking this action to reach the beachhead to our south," Evans continued. "They cannot be allowed to do so unhindered. Therefore the *Johnston*, in company with the *Heermann*, will attempt to delay the enemy as long as we are able."

There was silence on the bridge. Jack felt it extended throughout the ship, the sound of the *Johnston*'s engines, the passing ocean, and the flap of her ensign in the breeze suddenly loud on the bridge.

"Let's go get those bastards!" someone screamed from the lookout position. As if a finger had been taken from an emotional dyke, the *Johnston* broke out in a raucous series of shouts and curses. Evans exhaled, and Jack saw a moment of relief cross the commander's face.

I guess if there was ever a time a crew was going to mutiny, it'd be when we were almost certainly signing our own death warrants, Jack thought.

"Sir, engineering reports we are down to a little over an hour and a half of fuel at this speed," the bridge talker said.

Evans snorted. He gestured for Jack to come over.

"Tell Lieutenant Cochran I don't need any more updates on the fuel," Evans said lowly. "Only engineering casualties if we have any. If we're still afloat in ninety minutes then clearly the Lord will provide."

The roar of airplane engines caused Jack to look up. A flight of four, two *Avengers* escorted by a pair of *Wildcats*, came out of the low clouds. Circling *Johnston*, they identified her as a friendly, waggled their wings, then went back up into the clouds.

Poor bastards, Jack thought.

There was a low *whoomp!* As something exploded in the *St. Lo*'s hull. Jack watched as debris arced lazily upwards from the blast, the rushing wind rustling his uniform a few seconds later.

Then again, they may be the lucky ones who survive because they can run away.

3

A RUSH OF STINGING HORNETS

CATNIP LEADER
0635 LOCAL
25 OCTOBER

IT HAD BEEN ALMOST an hour since Aaron had launched from the *Gambier Bay* yet the radio net remained total chaos. Aaron had long given up trying to make sense of what was going on or what carriers survived. All he knew was that there were maybe ten aircraft now circling at four thousand feet around ten miles north of the black smoke columns that marked the death of at least two of Taffy 3's six carriers.

"Catnip Base, Catnip Base, this is Catnip Leader," Rizzo was saying urgently into the radio. "Please advise follow on forces that we are assembling near Point Minneapolis, I say again, Point Minneapolis."

Big to assume anyone made it off the deck after us, Aaron thought. Other than Rhodes, none of the six aircraft circling near what VC-10 had designated as Point Minneapolis were from *Gambier Bay*. Nor had he heard anyone calling from "Catnip Base" in the madness that was Taffy 3's net.

*I know the **White Plains** was done for, and I'm pretty sure I saw another ship turn turtle*, Aaron thought. *Those bastards probably figured out the range before we even knew they were there.*

"Sir, what are we going to do?" Rizzo asked from behind him. "I've been tracking the bastards better than earlier through this slop."

Who would have thought it'd all come down to a damn heavy box, a screen, and some cathode tubes? Aaron thought. Radar had been a wonder when he'd first been introduced to it a year ago, and the technology still sometimes confounded him. But if there was one thing he knew, it was that Rizzo could make the set do amazing things.

"All Taffy planes north of the Great Danes, this Catnip Leader," Aaron said. He watched a flight of four aircraft spiral up out of the cloud deck below as he talked. "Report in by section, let's see who we have."

It took five minutes due to the carriers and destroyers regularly breaking in. Aaron realized he had a pair of aircraft from the *Fanshaw Bay* (Bendix), the first division that had taken off from the ill-fated *White Plains* (Fido), and the late arriving flight from *Kalinin Bay* (Georgia). Two more minutes of conversation told him that at least eight more aircraft had gone on ahead and started attacking the Japanese without waiting for help.

Well, a pickup group is better than going it alone, Aaron thought. *Those bastards must have more balls than sense.*

"All right, let's get south and try to find something to bomb," he said. "Ceiling was at around 1,000 feet when we got up here. No need to drop down until we're about ten miles off the bastards. Georgia Lead, you go to their starboard, everyone else follow me in from port. Fighters, you go on ahead and strafe."

There were several acknowledgments over the crowded radio net. Then suddenly one call came through plain as day.

"All stations, all stations, Bendix Base is gone," a young, agitated voice said. "I say again, Bendix base is gone!"

Guess we won't be getting any more instructions from Rear Admiral Sprague, Aaron thought. He felt nauseous for a moment, swallowing hard past the lump in his throat.

"Sir, come to course one nine zero true," Rizzo said.

"Understood," Aaron replied. "Morgan, you awake back there?"

"Sir, I've never been more awake in my life," Morgan said. "I just don't think you want to hear me praying the Rosary for the fiftieth time."

"We've come this far, I don't intend to get us dead now," Aaron stated. "Wish we had a torpedo rather than those depth charges, but they'll do well enough for trying to start a fire or slow someone down."

Hope I sound more convincing than I feel, Aaron thought. The four 500-pound depth charges in his bomb bay were designed to plunge to a given depth and detonate from water pressure. A direct hit would likely skip right off a surface vessel's deck. Even with their shallowest setting, a more fortuitous near miss would do well to spring some leaks.

"I hope not, sir," Rizzo said. "I've got a gal back home I'm sweet on and it sure would break her heart to stop getting letters."

There, Aaron thought, suddenly seeing their quarry through a break in the clouds. The glimpse was small and gone almost as soon as it started. Still, he felt his stomach drop.

That's the biggest fucking battleship I've ever seen, he thought. *Looked like the damn Chrysler building on its side.*

"The good lieutenant's not going to let your only experience with a woman be some three minute rub and tug back on Oahu," Morgan muttered sarcastically, filling the silence. Despite the gravity of the situation, Aaron had to bite his lip to keep from laughing.

"You know, you promised you'd never…"

The sky was suddenly alive with flak. The black bursts were not particularly accurate, being off in elevation and speed, but there was plenty of it.

"Sir, I'm getting on my gun," Rizzo said.

"Roger Rizzo," Aaron replied. "You did a good job getting us steered on target."

"Thank you, sir!" Rizzo replied as he turned to the *Avenger*'s belly gun.

Once more Aaron came through the cloud, and the air was alive with colored smoke and tracers.

Ceiling is way too low for this shit, he thought. *We're practically on top of their guns!*

"All right gents, in we go," Aaron said over the radio. "Get that big cruiser at the front left of the formation!"

Wish I had a damn torpedo, he thought. *They're barely even zig zagging.* He opened the *Avenger*'s bomb bay doors as he lined up on the big heavy cruiser. The torpedo bomber shuddered as a flak burst exploded just off their starboard side, but miraculously without effect.

Fucking bastards! Aaron thought, briefly considering returning fire with the *Avenger*'s two forward firing machine guns. The speed of his approach made him reconsider, as it suddenly seemed like he'd shed several hundred feet in the blink of an eye. Jerking hard on the bomb release, Aaron began pulling out to avoid the intense flak. Only belatedly did he realize he'd pulled back on the stick a half second too soon.

That's gonna be a bad miss, he thought angrily, just as both

Rizzo and Morgan began firing backwards at the Japanese heavy cruiser. *Dammit, dammit, dammit!*

"Near miss, sir!" Rizzo said.

"That wasn't ours!" Morgan noted. "Oh Jesus, those poor bastards."

Aaron put the *Avenger* in a turn and looked back just in time to see what Morgan was talking about. Another *Avenger* was heading towards the water, inverted and smoking. Aaron turned away before the final impact, but Morgan's fervent cursing told him all he needed to know.

"Any Taffy 3 aircraft, any Taffy 3 aircraft, this is Banjo Leader," their radio crackled. "I have shackle jig unshackle aircraft, shackle george unshackle with pickles."

Aaron looked down at his pilot's board. "Banjo" was the code name for the U.S.S. *Natoma Bay*, flagship for Task Unit 77.4.2, or "Taffy Two." The word "shackle" told him to consult the "shackle code," a simple daily cipher that allowed friendly units to communicate numbers to one another. Each phonetic letter from the transmission could be quickly cross referenced to a corresponding letter.

Always thought it was paranoia to think that the Japanese were listening to our radio communications, Aaron thought. *But I would have also sworn I'd never see a Japanese battleship in combat yet here we are.*

Taking his hand briefly off the throttle, he quickly rotated the page…and started cursing as he looked at the date.

Shit shit shit!

Distracted by Rhodes' engine problems, he had forgotten to check his pilot's board. The code for *24 October* stared accusingly at him.

"Sir, you need the shackle code?" Rizzo asked from down below.

I'm getting this kid a promotion, Aaron thought. *He is always Johnny on the spot.*

"Yes Rizzo," he replied.

"He's got eight aircraft, four with torpedoes," Rizzo replied.

That's not going to go far at all, Aaron thought, thinking back to the storm of flak they'd just flown through. *But it's all we've got.*

"Catnip Leader, Catnip Two, I am guns dry," Rhodes' voice crackled across this speakers. Aaron jumped, having totally forgotten about his wingman. There was a quick series of check ins as other Taffy 3 aircraft began to report their ammunition status. Aaron took a deep breath.

"Rizzo, tell all Taffy aircraft with ammo to meet me at angels six," Aaron said. "Morgan, get green flares ready."

THE ENSUING COMMUNICATIONS CONSUMED FIVE MINUTES that seemed like an eternity and required six flares, but Aaron managed to get a hasty twelve aircraft strike organized. Through intermittent breaks in the cloud, Aaron could see the Japanese vessels firing occasionally off to the northeast.

*Well, it's at least a hopeful sign they have **something** to still be shooting at*, he thought. That was followed by a hard swallow as he considered how many of his friends could be dead or dying at the other end of those shells.

"Any change to their course or speed, Rizzo?" Aaron asked.

"None sir," Rizzo replied.

The arrogant bastards aren't even deviating from their way south, he thought. *We'll have to see what we can do about that.*

"Sir, it sounds like Taffy 1 is having a bit of a time of

it," Rizzo said. "I think I just heard someone report a submarine attack."

"Well if we don't slow these bastards down some there's going to be plenty more for them to worry about," Aaron replied.

He looked at his map.

"Not to mention poor Taffy 2," he muttered. If not for the rain, he was fairly certain the Japanese would already be able to range Rear Admiral Stump's task force.

If they come the slightest bit east of their heading, that is.

"All fighters, we should be just ahead of the ships," Aaron said. "On my mark, start your strafing runs."

There were a couple of acknowledgements over the radio, and he saw a circling *Wildcat* waggle its wings.

"Pickles, follow me down," Aaron said. "We'll try to set up an anvil on one of of the last two battleships."

"Uh, sir, what are we doing?" Morgan asked, his voice rising in pitch.

"What do you mean, Morgan?" Aaron asked.

"It sounds like we're leading a torpedo run without a torpedo," Morgan replied archly.

"Sailor, that's *exactly* what we're doing," Aaron snapped. "Last time I checked, I'm still in charge of this aircraft. So unless you'd like to step out, do your damn job without the commentary."

Aaron winced as soon as the words were out of his mouth. While it had always been clear that their aircraft was not a democracy, Aaron also tried to leave the door open for discourse. The other two men's lives were in his hands, and there had to be a certain degree of trust there. He'd watched other pilots, Murdock in particular, burn much of their goodwill by treating their aircrew just a step over servants.

And now here I am basically telling Morgan to shut up, I'm in charge here, Aaron thought.

"Aye aye, *sir*," Morgan replied.

"Catnip Leader, I've got about ten minutes of fuel left before I'll have to break off," a Taffy 2 *Avenger* pilots chimed in. "We need to get this show on the road."

What in the fuck did you do, leave with barely half your tank? Aaron thought angrily.

"Roger," Aaron replied. "Remember shackle codes."

"Understand," the pilot replied.

Aaron took one last look around the cloudy, squall-filled sky.

"Fighters, mark!" he barked, then put his own *Avenger* into a steady, diving turn.

With his eyes on his bank angle and instruments, Aaron had expected another four hundred feet before their *Avenger* broke into the open. The appearance of a Japanese heavy cruiser suddenly in front of him was startling, and that was *before* the big ship opened fire. Tracers seemed to move in a slow arc towards the *Avenger* before suddenly hurtling by on either side of the canopy.

Shit on a biscuit, they're getting **more** *accurate*, he thought. His assailant was a different cruiser than the one he'd bombed before, as he noted the all forward armament and clear aft deck.

Tone *or* **Chikuma**, he thought, then wondered briefly where that knowledge had come from. Shaking his head, he looked down at his speed as they hurtled past the vessel's stern.

I sure hope these bastards have the new shrouds for the torpedoes, he thought. *It'd be suicide to be making a run at early war speeds*.

"Fuck!" Morgan cried. "They got one of the other planes!"

Aaron gritted his teeth at the news. Seeing the fast-moving Japanese battleship before them, he skidded slightly just as its side erupted in smoke and fire. The impromptu maneuver saved his life, as a perfect row of 6-inch shell splashes appeared where their *Avenger* would have been flying.

This is insane! Aaron thought. His heart was thundering in his ears, time seeming to slow even though he knew the *Avenger* was doing well over a hundred knots. Once more flame lit up the Japanese battleship's side, and this time he actually heard the shells go just over his head with a sound like ripping canvas. Without taking his eyes off the battleship, he opened the *Avenger*'s bomb bay doors.

Gotta sell the dry run, he thought. *Have to make them believe we're about to put a damn pickle right in their side.*

Quickly swiveling his head, he saw that there was only one other *Avenger* remaining. The other aircraft was smoking slightly from its engine, holes visible in its fuselage and the rear gunner's turret shattered. But in that brief instant, Aaron and the other pilot locked gazes, the other man's eyes wide.

Drop any time, Aaron thought, waving, then turned back forward. A stream of tracers arced towards them, with several impacts shaking the stick in Aaron's hands.

"He dropped! He dropped!" Morgan screamed. Aaron didn't acknowledge, skidding his rudder and toggling the bomb bay doors closed. The Japanese battleship, a maritime colossus looming in front of him, was a mass of flame from her guns..

Wait, he's turning away from us, Aaron thought as they climbed away to the other side of the vessel. A flash of blue and roar of engine was the only warning they had that one of the starboard side *Avenger*s had also decided to head aft of the battleship. Before Aaron could react, the two aircraft were hurtling by each other in a buffet of slip stream and vibrations.

Oh God, Aaron thought, swinging his head around to see if there were any more aircraft heading directly at him. Fighting his unstable aircraft, Aaron put the *Avenger* into a steeper turn that brought his nose around to head away from the Japanese battleship at a roughly seventy degree angle. Out of the corner of his eye, a flaming comet that was once an *Avenger* slammed into the Japanese battleship's stern from the starboard side. The gout of fire and debris tumbled past the stern turrets, undoubtedly killing several of the warship's exposed crew as well as the three Americans aboard.

Got to get us out of here, he thought.

"Where's that other *Avenger*?" he asked.

There was only the sound of his engine and flak bursting around him as an answer.

"Goddammit," Aaron muttered. He started to lift up in his seat, then realized they were heading right for a maneuvering Japanese destroyer. Not wanting ot smash his own aircraft into the side of an enemy warship, Aaron forced thoughts of his impromptu wingman out of his head while clumsily maneuvering clear. For their part, the Japanese crew seemed to be surprised to see his aircraft, only a desultory few tracers zipping by.

"*Holy shit! Holy shit! We got her!*" Morgan screamed.

"What?" Aaron asked.

"She's hit! The Jap bitch is hit!"

Clear of the destroyer, Aaron pushed up and turned around in his seat to see what Morgan was talking about. He could see the telltale spout of a torpedo hit falling back into the ocean from the vessel's port side.

Fuck yes! Aaron thought.

. . .

The I.J.N.S. *Haruna*, like her sisters *Kongo*, *Hiei*, and *Kirishima*, had begun life as a battlecruiser in a much different era. The last of the four sisters to be constructed, she had been the first modified into a "fast battleship" in the interwar years. Unfortunately this modification had left a small, poorly armored portion of the hull near each vessel's steering room, with the IJN's naval architects assuming it was far too small to be struck in combat except by a lucky hit. Despite *Hiei* being crippled by a proverbial "Golden BB" from an American heavy cruiser that holed the location, the IJN had never considered fixing the error. The *Kongo*-class were far too valuable and needed to lay up in the yard for the necessary months, and such an incident happening again would be the equivalent of cleaning out a casino twice in one night.

The young ensign from the U.S.S. *Manila Bay* had not been an avid gambler. Indeed, any claims to being "lucky" would have been seemingly disproven by the the 25mm shell that had shredded his thoracic cavity as he broke past the *Haruna*'s stern. Still, if there was an afterlife, the single Mark 13 torpedo he dropped began a chain of consequences that would swiftly began adding to the queue that was almost assuredly forming outside Valhalla's gates that particular morning. Unlike her sister, *Haruna* was swiftly and summarily crippled by the 600-pounds of Torpex killing every single officer and rating inside the steering room. The blast simultaneously shattered the generators used to provide power to the massive vessel's rudder and severed the ability to manual shift the control surface.

Forward and above the wound, the vessel's helmsman screamed in dismay as the battleship suddenly began to reverse her turn. Despite the immediate and sharp intervention of the vessel's captain, followed by a petty officer grabbing the wheel, the out of control *Haruna*'s bow continued to swing around and careen towards her escorts.

"Sir, let's get out of here!" Morgan shouted. The cry caused Aaron to break out of staring at the obviously damaged Japanese battleship.

"Hold on, we have to get a damage report!" Aaron replied. "Rizzo, get ready to send in…"

Aaron never really heard the blast or blasts. The human brain had a way of dampening senses in the face of great, chaotic trauma. For this reason the cacophony of sound that occurred as a heavy anti-aircraft shell burst just within lethal range of the *Avenger* was somewhat muted. The rush of air and whine of fragments told him that something *bad* had happened, and Morgan's screaming indicated it was bad enough to have hurt the entire aircraft. But terrifyingly, the fact he could not breathe due to the acrid, cloying aroma of burnt powder and the dropping sensation of the *Avenger* was the most pressing sensation.

Hit…we're hit, he thought, instinctively fighting to bring the bomber back to level trim. As he did so, the world came rushing back with great violence, Morgan's cries decreasing in volume and increasing in profanity. The *Avenger* reacted sluggishly, but thankfully did not start into a spin. A quick glance told him that despite its rough sound and obvious damage, the engine continued to run. The canopy was holed in many places, and Aaron realized half of his instruments were now useless.

"Crew, report," he said, the sound coming out in barely a whisper. He tried to swallow, and immediately regretted it as the *taste* of gunpowder filled his mouth. Aaron fought to get his canteen to his mouth as he staggered the aircraft away from the Japanese task force. To his surprise, no more fire came towards them… and then they were in a rain squall. Giving up on the canteen, he put his mouth towards the driving rain and opened it, the water giving him some degree of moisture to swish then spit.

Thank god the artificial horizon is still working, he thought, even as rain pelted him in the face. *This is bad enough I'd probably crash.*

"Crew, report!" Aaron reported, this time clearly audible. There was silence.

Shit, Aaron thought. *I killed them.* Turning to try and look aft, Aaron belatedly realized he had wet himself..

"Sir…" Morgan breathed out after a couple of minutes. "Rizzo is dead!"

"What?"

"What do you mean, 'what,' you stupid son-of-a-bitch?" Morgan said, still crying and obviously distraught. "Half his damn head is gone and he's bleeding like a freshly chopped chicken all over the compartment."

Goddammit, Aaron thought. He felt hot tears starting to form in his eyes, so he closed them briefly.

"Morgan, get a hold of yourself," he snapped, reopening them

There was a long silence from the back of the aircraft.

"Are you injured?" Aaron asked, putting the *Avenger* on a southerly heading.

I hope Taffy 2 is still somewhat in this direction and not just running for it straight, he thought, looking at the fuel gauge. It was obvious one of the tanks had been holed, as the needle was much lower than what could be accounted for by combat.

The self-sealing must have worked or we'd be dead, he thought.

"Yes, *sir*, I am," Morgan replied. "I got gashed on the

back of my shoulder, but I don't think I'm still bleeding, *sir*. I would ask Rizzo to look at it, but as I mentioned, he's *dead, sir*."

Aaron took a deep breath, then let it out.

I killed his best friend, Aaron thought. *I'd be upset too, and shouting at him doesn't do any good.*

"Morgan, I am sorry," Aaron said, shocked at how much weariness and anguish was in his voice. "I cannot bring him back. But we have to find someplace to land, and I need your help with that."

There was a long silence, the duration of which made Aaron start to panic that Morgan had been hit worse hit than he realized.

"Sir, you need to do right by Rizzo," Morgan said. "He kept a picture of that girl and her latest letter in his survival gear. If we make it, you need to write her a letter. Make it sound like Rizzo died the biggest badass this side of Oahu."

Aaron exhaled in relief.

"I can do that," he replied. "I give you my word."

"Good," Morgan said. "Now let's find us a damn flight deck.

USS WASHINGTON
0645 LOCAL

"SIR, VICE ADMIRAL HALSEY *HIMSELF* IS NOW ASKING FOR our position."

The words hung in the flag combat information center (CIC). Whereas the *Washington*'s CIC was the nerve center for the battleship, the flag CIC performed that function for the entire task force. It was rare for it to be dead silent like a church, but the staff officer's statement had made the atmosphere completely funereal.

Well, guess someone's about to make choices, Orrick thought. *But there's no eyepatch or eyepiece here.* He was sitting roughly five feet from Lee at the side of the map, a copy of the Office of Naval Intelligence's latest Japanese fleet handbook in his hand.

Too bad there's no instructions for how to make a time machine out of all these electronics in this handbook, Orrick thought grimly. *Because we're late to a murder.*

Vice Admiral Lee didn't even look up from where he was looking at the map. The man was tapping his fingers as he worked out whether Task Force 34 could cut any corners to close the distance with the Japanese ahead of them.

"Sir…" Commodore Jeter interjected, waving off the lieutenant commander who had relayed Third Fleet's initial inquiry.

"Maintain radio silence," Lee snapped. "Did the *Santa Fe* get that seaplane launched?"

"Yes sir," Jeter replied.

"Good, then Third Fleet staff will have the answer in probably another thirty minutes," Lee stated. "If they'd answered our questions last night, we'd be answering theirs already *because we'd be in goddamn range*."

I have not seen him this pissed since I've been aboard, Orrick thought. *Of course, he knows men are dying as we speak.*

It had taken another two hours past the estimated time for *South Dakota* to jury rig a fix for her engineering casualty. As he wasn't a snipe himself, Orrick did not quite understand what the problem was. He just sincerely hoped it was something that a competent "black gang" would have been expected to catch.

I'm not **sure** *Lee can hang someone from the yardarm*, Orrick thought. *But I know he's angry enough to try.*

Lee stabbed out a cigarette.

"Any word from Seventh Fleet?" he asked.

"No sir," Jeter replied. "Their command net seems to be a mess."

"Panic will do that to someone," Lee muttered angrily. "Damn Kinkaid."

To be fair, if I'd had a bunch of battleships just show up to my north I might be pissing my pants as well, Orrick thought. *Sure feel sorry for whomever is the intelligence officer on that staff.*

Jeter furrowed his brows.

"Sir, I just realized: Seventh Fleet has no idea we are coming south," the chief of staff stated. He gestured vaguely towards the hatch forward of flag CIC. "We should probably mention to someone there's about to be an unfamiliar capital ship and a pair of heavy cruisers coming from the north."

Lee shook his head vehemently.

"No," Lee snapped." We will give the Japanese no warning we're here," Lee snapped. He seemed about to say more when he staggered, briefly reaching towards the left side of his chest before grabbing the table instead.

That's not good. That's not good at all.

"Sir, you should probably have a seat," Jeter said, worriedly. Lee looked like he wanted to argue, but then nodded and sat down. Even in the CIC's less than ideal lighting, Orrick could see that the man's face was pale. Orrick turned towards a nearby runner.

"Get the flag surgeon," he stated quietly.

"Sir?" the young man asked, confused.

"The. Surgeon. Get him, *now*," Orrick stated vehemently. "Quietly, but move."

"Aye aye, sir," the sailor replied, slipping from the compartment.

Doesn't look as bad as Dad did, but I'd wager a hundred dollars that man is about to have a heart attack, Orrick thought. His father had dropped dead two minutes into the father-daughter dance at his eldest sister's wedding. Allegedly even if it had happened on a hospital floor there would have been nothing anyone could have done, but Orrick had familiarized himself with the signs of a heart attack from that day on.

"Sir, the Commander of Taffy 2 is reporting he is now under fire."

"Goddammit," Jeter shouted, then caught himself, taking a sharp breath. "Give the old man time to think, gentlemen."

Lee gripped the edge of the table and continued to stare at the chart.

"Orrick, what the hell is going on?" Lieutenant Commander Bridges, the admiral's surgeon, muttered as he appeared beside Orrick. "Some scared sailor said you told him to come get...oh shit."

Bridges quickly unsnapped his doctor's bag, and Orrick could see no further explanation was needed. Reaching in to grab a pill bottle, the surgeon looked at Lee nervously.

"How long has he been like that?" Bridges asked.

"A few minutes," Orrick replied.

"Make a hole!" Bridges said lowly, pushing forward through men rushing to and fro. Jeter, seeing who had disturbed the staff's flow, stepped forward to meet the surgeon. For his part, Orrick moved back towards the desk that held all the traffic that was coming in from the Seventh Fleet task groups. Picking up the first sheets, he quickly scanned them.

"This one here, from the *Johnston*," he said. "How old is it?"

"Just got it a few minutes ago, sir," the haggard ensign reading the traffic replied.

"Does the plot reflect?" he asked.

"Not yet, sir," the man replied, pausing before the last word. Orrick could see the poor ensign was not keeping up with the sheer number of messages Seventh Fleet was passing in clear text.

Like a frightened woman being chased down by a crazed killer who stops to use a payphone to call the police then starts spouting gibberish, Orrick thought angrily. *'We're aware there's a killer, Madam, but what's the address.'*

"I'll bring this right back," Orrick said. He headed towards where Vice Admiral Lee was just getting to his feet. Commander Jeter gave him a hard look as he was helping the admiral steady himself.

"Sir, we'll come get you the minute there's contact," Jeter was saying quietly. "Just let the meds do their job."

Who is going to take over if he is unable to continue? Orrick thought. *Hell, who do we have who **can** take over in this situation?*

USS JOHNSTON
0705 LOCAL

"Sir, radar confirms two big skunks moving at heading one six five true at ten knots, range one seven thousand. The rest of the big ones are proceeding one eight zero true at twenty knots and accelerating."

Radar is an amazing invention, Jack thought, palms sweaty as he listened to the report from CIC. *But looking at the old man, it's about to get me killed.*

Johnston had spent the last forty-five minutes chasing the large Japanese ships as they'd pounded their way south. The increasingly heavy rain squalls had largely hidden the small destroyer, which explained how they'd manage to close just over 17,000 yards without getting smashed to pieces. Well, that and the Japanese inexplicably circling for fifteen minutes.

Still wonder what made them stop, Jack thought. *But I guess that doesn't matter now.* He'd just returned to the bridge from engineering, where the destroyer's "black gang" were trying to create miracles and eke more steaming time out of the low oil remaining in her tanks.

"Okay, it's starting to get lighter," Evans said, looking out the bridge's forward window.

"Sir, guns says he has visibility on enemy vessels!" the talker said, his voice starting to rise with nervousness.

"Bring her back around to get us into that squall," Evans said. "Hard maneuver, helm!"

Jack braced himself as the *Johnston* heeled over to port. Two minutes passed at most before several lines of splashes appeared where the destroyer would have been if she'd kept going.

Apparently they dye their heavy shells just like we do, Jack thought, pulse racing at the tall columns that were higher than *Johnston*'s mast.

"Order the engine room to make smoke," Evans said, then nodded at Jack. "Also inform them that Ensign Murphy has passed his word about us being low on chemicals."

After we burn the chemical smoke, we'll have to do it with our own oil, Jack thought. *Which just decreases our range.*

"Okay, we know where they are, they now know where we are," Evans said. "Or where they think we are." He gestured for the sound powered phone.

"Guns, what'd you see?" he asked. There was a couple

minute pause that saw Evans nodding several times at Lieutenant Hagen's report from the *Johnston*'s director.

"Looks like the damn airedales did something good for once," Evans said, grinning like a man who'd just seen their wife's fleeing paramour fall and break their ankle. "If she's down by the stern and barely making steerage, we can kill her."

Jack could hear Hagen's excited tone clearly through the sound phone even if he couldn't make out the words.

"Yes, we could shoot radar and probably hit her," Evans replied. "But we've got to turn those other heavy ships around before they shoot the shit out of Taffy 2. We're not going to pull that off without coming out of the smoke."

Taffy 2 can take care of their damn selves, Jack thought. He'd heard the frantic radio conversations as he'd passed the communications compartment. The Japanese heavy ships had begun firing from 20,000 yards on Taffy 2's flattops, driving the other task force further east. Thankfully the worsening weather, which was probably already wreaking havoc with flight operations, had also been harming their accuracy.

Or at least I didn't hear anything that sounded like this morning's insanity, Jack thought. *Pretty sure none of them actually got hit*.

"We'll launch at ten thousand yards," Evans continued. "Figure out a way to pass word to the individual mounts from radar in case you're hit."

With that, *Johnston*'s master handed the sound powered phone back to the talker and resumed his position behind the helmsman.

"Tell the *Heermann* she'll also fire on the battleship," Evans said. "Guns on smaller vessels, we're not going to do a damn thing to a battleship's hide at this range."

"Aye aye, sir."

Evans looked up at he clock.

"We turn out of the squall in five minutes," he stated. "1MC."

Jack listened to the chatter from the radio room as a dead silence fell over the bridge. It appeared three or four smaller Japanese ships were starting to head to where *Johnston* had been, their relative bearing off the destroyer's starboard quarter.

They can't see us through the squall, Jack thought. *That won't last when we turn in.* He quickly did the geometry and time factors in his head. The *Johnston* would have to cover roughly eight thousand yards to launch her ten fish. At a speed of thirty-six knots, that was somewhere between five and ten minutes. The torpedoes, in turn, would take roughly that long to reach the Japanese battleship.

There's no way we make that, Jack thought. *Not with three ships plus what sounds like three destroyers all shooting at us.* Commander Evans startled him out of his grim calculus.

"Men, this is the captain," Evans began. "The Japanese continue to press on to attack Taffy 2. The aviators have crippled a battleship, what appears to be a *Kongo*-class."

Eight 14-inch guns, Jack thought, recalling the Naval Intelligence book he'd studied every night since commissioning. *Over a dozen 6-inchers. That's almost twenty guns that can kill us in an instant.*

"The Bible tells us the Israelites, on the eve of David's battle with Goliath, were deeply afraid," Evns continued. "The Philistines had made it very clear what fate awaited them if David lost, and all this unknown boy had was a rock."

If this talk is trying to make us feel better…

"Well, gentlemen, our guns aren't going to do a thing

to that battleship," Evans said. "But we've got something better than a rock, and ten of them to boot."

Jack looked up from the plot to see Evans looking at him. The commander smirked.

"Some of you, no doubt, have heard our torpedoes are junk," Evans began.

Holy shit, he remembered last night, Jack thought surprised.

"But as two Jap battleships found out last night, they work *just fine,*" Evans continued. "And unlike those fellows on the destroyers last night, we don't have a battleline to split the credit with."

Fucking Halsey, Jack thought. *For that matter, fucking Kinkaid.*

"We're about to go in here and write a chapter in naval history that will get us mentioned in the same breath as John Paul Jones and Cushing," Evans stated, his tone firm. "I told you when I took this ship we would go into harm's way. Well she's certainly swift, and we're about to do some giant slaying. I am proud of every man aboard this vessel, and I look forward to not having to buy another drink in Honolulu after we get back to Pearl. Godspeed."

Turning off the intercom, Evans shouted back into the radar plot.

"Bearing to the big skunk?"

"Zero seven oh, sir," came the reply.

"Signal the *Heermann* 'attack, attack, attack,'" Evans said.

Jack realized much of his fear had gone as Evans gave his orders to the helm. Bracing himself as the destroyer leaned to port against her sharp turn to starboard, Jack watched mounts 51 and 52, the two forward guns, continued to swing at what he assumed were the Japanese destroyers now off their starboard bow.

"Anytime guns wants to engage those Japanese tin cans, he may," Evans said.

The words were hardly out of his mouth before the firing gong sounded. Even as the rain was thinning, the forward guns began to speak.

The four closest Japanese destroyers were all members of Destroyer Squadron 10, commanded by Rear Admiral Susumi Kimura in the light cruiser *Yahagi*. With *Yahagi* alongside to assist *Haruna*, while *Nowaki* and *Kiyoshimo* helped to fend off the Americans' continued, disjointed air attacks, Kimura had assumed four *Kagero*-class destroyers (*Hamakaze*, *Isokaze*, *Urakaze*, and *Yukikaze*) would be more than a match for a single American destroyer.

Had conditions been normal or his lookouts' reports correct, Kimura would have been quite correct. Unfortunately for his four subordinates, they were fighting two destroyers they could not see in the poor visibility. Apart from the battleships and a couple of the heavy cruisers, none of the IJN's vessels even possessed radar, much less radar capable of blind fire. In contrast, both *Heermann* and *Johnston*'s radars not only provided accurate range and bearing to their Japanese counterparts, but were mated to excellent fire control computers in the destroyers' plotting rooms.

Hamakaze, leading the column of four Japanese destroyers, was engaged at just over 7,000 yards by *Heermann*. Beginning with two gun salvoes, *Heerman*'s gunnery officer trusted in his bearing and ranges even without clear sight of his target. From the Japanese perspective, the squall and gloom off their starboard bow suddenly began to flash with a pair of shells every ten to twelve seconds. Even as her lookouts screamed out a warning, *Heermann*'s fourth salvo put a shell into the destroyer's forwardmost turret. Secondary explosions and fragments from this first hit scythed down exposed crew in the vessel's superstructure. Moments later, two shells in the fifth salvo detonated in the *Hamakaze*'s machinery spaces. The *Heerman's* gunnery officer, suddenly presented with a clear picture as his vessel exited the squall, took a short pause for all five of his guns to be loaded, then began slamming full five-gun salvoes into her opponent.

Watching the disaster that befell her sister ship directly ahead, the *Isokaze* just barely avoided the same fate by putting her helm hard over to port. *Johnston*'s first salvo, all five guns, thus fell twenty yards short. With *Hamakaze* slowing and drunkenly swinging to starboard, the *Isokaze*'s fire was fouled as her gunnery officer tried to track onto *Hermann*. *Johnston*, on the other hand, was a full ship's length behind her companion and had no such concerns. Hapless *Hamakaze* stopped one of the *Johnston*'s 5-inch shells with her bridge, her captain and most of the structure's occupants killed by the hit. The four remaining ones somehow passed over and around *Hamakaze* on their way to *Isokaze*. One missed forward, the other short, but the the remaining pair hit the oxygen generator for the *Hamakaze*'s torpedo battery.

"KEEP HITTING HER! KEEP HITTING HER!" EVANS shouted, his binoculars up to his face. Jack, standing on the bridge wing, had his own glasses hanging around his neck.

Damn forward guns can't track, he thought, seeing the two guns in question hard against their stays.

The ragged salvo that landed all around them sent fragments rattling off the superstructure. Screams from behind him told Jack that at least two lookouts had been hit.

"Dammit, her sisters are joining in," Evans muttered. "Zizag pattern three, we can't dodge their shots individually."

"Zigzag pattern three, aye-aye," the helmsman replied. *Johnston* began weaving and bobbing as three of the Japanese destroyers began. There was a dull crash aft and the *Johnston* shuddered.

"Hit in the port 20mm mount, sir," the talker said, face draining of color. "The mount is destroyed."

Likely got the crew as well, Jack thought.

Evans strode to the port side and looked aft, then crossed the bridge to the other side.

"*Heermann*'s giving one of those destroyers the business!" he observed happily.

In reality, *Heermann* had given *two* of their assailants "the business." *Hamakaze*, like a streetfighter surprised by a blunt object to the forehead, had staggered out of the fight and into the rain squall that had once hid *Heermann*. Desperately fighting the fires raging in her torpedo flats, the vessel was obviously a temporary, if not permanent, mission kill. Correctly assessing that the blazing IJN DD was out of it and *Johnston* could no longer bear on the *Isokaze*, *Heermann* had stopped her own headlong charge towards *Haruna* in order to finish off the second DD.

Had it been two years prior, off the Solomons, *Isokaze*'s crew would have likely made her American counterpart pay for her temerity. Unfortunately for the Japanese destroyer, almost three years of war, oil shortages that prevented training, and almost forty-eight hours of unrelenting combat had slowed her crew's reaction times. By contrast, *Heermann* was manned by a well-trained, well-maintained and, most importantly, *fresh* crew. In less time than it took an average reader to finish a newspaper article, her main battery put eight shells into the *Isokaze*'s hull. Listing, with fires starting to blossom from her second funnel aft, the *Isokaze* also turned sharply away from *Heermann*.

Unfortunately for the USN destroyer, her crew were collectively guilty of one of combat's carnal sins: target fixation. Although initially just as surprised as their sister vessels, the *Urakaze*, and *Yukikaze* had enough time to get over their initial shock, come about, and finally begin firing at both USN destroyers. *Yukikaze*, with a far more veteran crew than any of her sisters, was the first to draw blood on the *Heermann* with two hits in the destroyer's stern. Although the American destroyer reacted with great alacrity, *Yukikaze* landed two more hits before the *Heermann* shifted fire. Both of these slowed the *Heermann*, allowing *Urakaze* to also find the range.

"GET THE REAR SHIP, GUNS!" EVANS SHOUTED INTO THE microphone, straining to be heard over the din of the main battery and, surprisingly, the 40-millimeter Bofors.

Those destroyers are much closer than I realized, Jack thought with terror. He continued looking forward, towards the battleship and cruiser on the horizon. Another line of squalls was moving from their starboard to port, threatening to get between *Johnston* and the two distant vessels.

"Sir, do we need to come about to help the *Heermann*?" Lieutenant Digardi asked.

"No!" Evans replied. "Keep us heading for the batt…"

With a sound like ripping canvas, the sea *erupted* around the *Johnston*. Four towering, black-tinged columns surrounded the destroyer, the water falling back and drenching the *Johnston*'s superstructure.

She straddled us, Jack thought, as his heart tried to claw its way out of his chest. *That bitch straddled us on her first salvo*.

"Murphy, tell me where the *Heermann* is!" Evans shouted, jolting Jack back to reality.

"Aye aye, sir!" Jack yelled back. Ears ringing from the *Johnston*'s own gunfire, he stepped onto the starboard wing of the bridge. His shoes crunched on something, and he looked down to see sand swept over a large bloodstain.

Is that all I'll be soon? he wondered. *A bloodstain?*

"Starboard twenty-degree rudder, all ahead flank!" Evans barked from behind him. "Main battery, engage that light cruiser!"

"Aye-aye, sir!" the helmsman replied, spinning the wheel. Evans picked up the talker as the *Johnston*'s guns swiveled towards the distant light cruiser. The air above the barrels seem wavered from the heat coming off each gun. Then they fired, and Jack's uniform rustled with the blast. Jack shook his head, then remembered why he had come to the starboard side.

Where are you? he thought as he raised his binoculars. *Oh, there*.

"Sir, *Heermann* is at bearing one six oh!" he called across the bridge to Evans just as the main battery fired again. Turning to study their sister ship again, Jack cursed as he realized the *Heermann* was falling behind, steam starting to issue from her amidships. The other destroyer began to turn to port, and Jack gritted his teeth as he got a good look at her aft end.

She took a major hit, he thought as *Heerman*'s torpedo mounts began disgorging their deadly loads. *Looks hurt bad, probably the battleship's secondaries*.

"Sir, *Heermann* is launching torpedoes!" he shouted.

"Guns, is that BB moving yet?" Evans asked, bringing up his own binoculars. "She looks like she's making a little headway, but not more than ten kno...*oh shit!*"

Through his own binoculars, Jack saw the same thing that had caused Evans to curse. *Haruna* had let fly with a full broadside, the massive cloud of smoke from her main guns briefly shrouding the battleship's upper works.

Oh God, he thought. Long seconds passed...then he realized the shells weren't aimed at *Johnston*. He looked aft just in time to see *Heermann* hit by at least two, if not three, shells. The exact count would never be known, as the impacts detonated the destroyer's forward magazines. Even half empty, there was more than enough ordinance to obliterate the vessel's forward half in a massive, distinctive fireball. Jack's stomach flip-flopped at the sight, and he had to swallow hard to avoid throwing up.

That...that had to be dumb luck, he thought. *They've been missing us all afternoon. How did they hit **Heermann** like that?* Shaking his head, Jack remembered he had a job to do.

"Sir, the *Heermann* has been hit!" he shouted. "They got her forward magazines!"

Evans looked over at Jack, his face set in a grimace. He nodded, waving the younger officer off, then nodded as he listened to what Jack assumed was Hagen repeating the grim news about the *Heermann*.

"Come to starboard, head us for that squall!" Evans barked into the pilothouse, pointing. The helmsman turned the wheel once more, with *Johnston*'s bow swinging sharply around to the new course. A few seconds later, two neat rows of shells landed roughly four hundred yards off the destroyer's port side.

"Enemy destroyers turning away!" a lookout called.

Bastards don't want to foul the battleship's range, Jack thought numbly. He stepped out onto the bridge wing again, bringing his binoculars up to look at the Japanese DDs. Then, like the hand of Providence itself, the *Johnston* was once more shrouded in rain.

"Range to that BB?" Evans asked.

"Eight thousand yards, captain!" someone in CIC shouted back.

Jack could see the captain musing, doing mental geometry in his head.

We need to just launch our torpedoes and leave, sir, Jack quietly willed. Seeing Evans purse his lips, Jack felt his nausea only increase.

"The most important part of gambling, gentlemen," Evans began, "is knowing when to quit."

Johnston's master grabbed the sound phone after a long pause.

"Guns, radar solution, fire torpedoes when ready."

"Aye aye, captain. Lining up…"

The squall was suddenly gone just as quickly as it had shrouded them.

Shit.

Jack immediately saw two things. One, the Japanese light cruiser was much, much closer and steaming directly at the *Johnston* from her port bow. Second, the cruiser was under air attack, a flight of F4Fs strafing her.

"Hard to starboard! Guns, get that cruiser!"

Evans' second command was superfluous, as *Johnston*'s main battery was already swiveling towards their assailant. At only 5,000 yards, even her shells had a chance to penetrate the other vessel's hull. Jack listened as the CIC crew began dealing with the changed threat, seeing the Japanese cruiser's forward turrets turning towards *Johnston*. Time seemed to slow, even as the destroyer's main battery fired first.

Just missed, Jack thought, the five splashes perfectly bracketing the *Yahagi*.

The flash from *Yahagi*'s guns and sound of ripping canvas of shells passing by were nearly simultaneous. Unfortunately for the Japanese cruiser, her gunnery officer had underestimated just how fast *Johnston* was closing with her. Then the 5-inch guns were firing again and with the 40mm Bofors joined in. Jack heard someone shout about having to recalculate the torpedo data for the battleship and Evans reply with an order about the spread…then all hell broke loose.

The bright flash of the *Yahagi* and *Haruna*'s fire arriving simultaneously nearly blinded Jack even as the concussion flung him across the bridge like he was a terrier caught in a hurricane. The breath whooshed out of his lungs as his side met the unyielding pilot house bulkhead with the sharp *crack* of several ribs breaking. Too stunned to be grateful he'd been wearing his steel helmet, Jack tried to take a breath and found his nose full of the stink of cordite.

"Fire! Fire in the CIC!" someone screamed from below, the report only barely intelligible over the din of screaming and dying men. Chest afire, Jack staggered to his feet and looked into the pilot house at the helm. For a moment it seemed like the helmsman was fine…until Jack realized the man's right leg was a pulsing stump. With a breathy sigh, the man let go of the wheel and dropped to the deck.

"Corpsman!" someone shouted from the deck below. "Corpsmen to the bridge!"

"Flooding in engine room 1!" another voice cried. "Fire aft!"

Jesus, our luck ran out all at once, Jack thought, trying to gain his bearings.

"Murphy, take the wheel!" Commander Evans

shouted. Jack was about to protest when he realized only Evans and he were still able to stand. The *Johnston* was steering in a circle with no one at the helm, a sure recipe for disaster.

Gotta grab that wheel or we're all going to die! The surge of adrenaline cleared his head even as the ringing in his ears remained. Staggering back into the pilothouse, Jack grabbed the destroyer's controls.

"Hard to port or that battleship is going to blow us to hell!" Evans barked.

Jack threw the rudder over. With a sense of relief, he realized the *Johnston* was still nimbly answering the helm.

"Mount fifty-two is gone, sir!"

Jack didn't recognize the speaker's voice, but was startled to realize the 5-inch turret in question was split open like tin can dropped on a bandsaw. Black smoke wafted out of the torn open roof, then was blown aft just below the pilothouse windows by the wind of *Johnston*'s passage. Jack could see lumps inside the turret that he belatedly realized were the charred bodies of his shipmates. Before his mind fully processed what he was seeing, another salvo of 6-inch shells bracketed the *Johnston*.

Shit...shit...SHIT!

"Sir, gunnery asks you hold her steady just for a few seconds more!" a runner shouted from the bridge wing. "The sound phone is out in the director!"

Before Evans could respond, there was a bright flash on the *Yahagi*'s superstructure followed by three waterspouts in the cruiser's vicinity. Motion drew Jack's eyes up, and he saw the hurtling shape of an *Avenger* ducking back into the clouds. Seconds later, the Japanese cruiser's broadside fired, the salvo over a hundred yards past the *Johnston*.

"Steady on the helm!" Evans barked. The runner nodded, then turned to begin the climb back up to the gunnery director high in *Johnston*'s superstructure. Jack looked up at *Haruna*'s large, hulking form. The battleship had gained even more speed, but was still moving in a straight line.

She's got to be having rudder problems, Jack thought. *She's almost a drill target without any maneuvering.*

The battleship's forward turrets belched fire and flame. For a horrible moment, Jack's brain convinced him he saw the massive shells in flight… then the *Johnston* shook as they exploded astern.

"Hope guns gets that solution set up in about sixty seconds…" Evans muttered. Jack gripped the wheel, fighting the urge to duck as *Yahagi*'s secondaries put shells just off the *Johnston*'s bow.

Hurry up! Hurry up!

"Sir, I will take the wheel!" a petty officer shouted over the 5-inch guns' din. Jack nodded, stepping to the side.

"Left full rudder!" Evans said. "Let's get back into that smoke! Murphy, get me a damage report from Battle Two!"

"Aye aye, sir!" Jack replied.

We might get out of here yet! he thought, heading for the hatch. He had just stepped out onto the starboard bridge wing when his world suddenly went black.

THE *JOHNSTON*'S FINAL TORPEDO SALVO JOINED *Heermann*'s, making a total of twenty torpedoes heading towards the crippled, accelerating *Haruna*. As Jack had noted, the damaged battleship was not turning at all. What neither he nor any other American could realize was that this was by unfortunate, but necessary design. *Hiei* had died off of Guadalcanal in part because her rudders had locked in a turn, making her all but unnavigable before American aircraft had set upon her. While the designers had not considered reinforcing the *Kongo*-class' Achilles' heel, they *had* fixed that problem. Alas, "fixing" in this case had meant placing a giant mechanical ram in place to literally knock either of the *Haruna*'s massive rudders into the amidships position.

Thus, even as she raised speed and increased steam, the *Haruna* was left unable to take the most prudent action: turning away from the oncoming wakes headed towards her across the turbulent sea. Like the fingers of outspread, malevolent hands, first the *Heermann*'s then the *Johnston*'s torpedoes came into easy view as they closed the last few thousand yards towards their prey. Ignoring the distant, damaged destroyers, the *Haruna*'s secondary, then anti-aircraft guns and, finally, in a fit of desperation, her main battery all fired towards the tin fish at the head of those wakes.

THE SENSATION OF BEING TUGGED FOLLOWED BY SHARP, terrible pain in his leg jarred Jack back into consciousness. The sound of crackling flames, roaring steam, and screaming men was thankfully dim.

I guess I'm not dead, he thought with great effort. Jack had never had a concussion before, but from the difficulty he was having in forming higher thought told him that was no longer the case.

"Sir, sir, ya gotta help me," a voice said in his ear. "I can't drag you much further."

Looking up, Jack saw the speaker had brown skin the color of mahogany and a thin, wiry build.

Mess steward, he thought. *Must have been on one of the casualty teams.*

"Have..have to get to Battle Two," Jack muttered. He

kicked out with his leg and immediately regretted it, as more searing pain shot up his lower body. He glanced down to see his right leg off at a horrid angle, the left seared like a Christmas turkey left in the oven too long. His uniform pants were mostly gone from mid-thigh down, with the remaining fragment charred.

Oh God, that looks bad, he thought,

"Battle Two ain't there, sir!" the steward shouted, his Southern accent thick. "We gotta get you into a float or you're going to die."

It was then Jack realized the *Johnston*'s deck was tilted, her bow up out of the water. Even through his diminished hearing he could hear steam escaping from somewhere belowdecks.

This ship is going to sink!

Sudden adrenaline coursed through him, and he got his left leg under him despite the red-hot agony the movement caused.

"What happened?" he asked. "Where's the captain?"

"Dead," the steward said. "Looks like that damn battleship hit the bridge. I think everyone's dead there. We found you draped near the forward torpedo mount."

Holy shit, Jack thought. Whatever had happened to the *Johnston*'s bridge had tossed him a few dozen feet aft. Which probably meant that everyone forward of the bridge was likely either dead or cut off from the rest of the vessel.

Damn lucky I landed on the deck and not in the water, he thought. Another staggering step and the resultant pain convinced him "lucky" might not be the correct word. His vision swam for a moment, his sense of balance off kilter as the ship made a strange motion. A plane roared overhead, and he looked up to see a *Wildcat* descending to strafe something aft of the *Johnston*, brass casings falling from the stubby fighters' wings.

"Corpsman!" someone shouted from behind him and the steward. "Jesus Christ, stop trying to walk ensign!"

It took a moment for Jack to realize the man was shouting about him. Looking aft at *Johnston*'s wrecked stern, he realized the man might have a point. A few moments later, he was getting lowered to the deck.

"Sir, there's going to be a bit of a pinch," said a corpsman he didn't recognize but looked hardly older than seventeen. Before Jack could respond, the man had jabbed him with a morphine syringe.

"*Got the bitch!*" someone screamed from aft of their position. Jack turned to see a shirtless, tattooed petty officer from one of the torpedo mounts, his arm in a sling, standing on what was left of a 40mm mount, binoculars in hand.

CONTRARY TO THE EXCLAMATION FROM THE *JOHNSTON*'S rapidly settling hulk, the first torpedo hit was from the *Heermann*'s salvo, not hers. Even with *Haruna*'s crippled condition, the *Heermann*'s salvo had been launched at long range and in extremis. As such, while not quite miraculous, that one of her torpedoes to hit was not so much "low percentage" as "lucky enough to get the entire torpedo department banned from Atlantic City for life."

Fortunately for the *Haruna*, the American destroyer's good fortune largely ended there. With her previous flooding, the battleship was low in the water. The slow running Mark XV thus expended the majority of its fury against the forward portion of the armored belt, with the primary impact being further flooding on the already damaged port side. It was not enough a fatal hit by any means, but it did serve to retard the *Haruna*'s already sluggish acceleration.

THE AIREDALES ARE AT LEAST GIVING THOSE DESTROYERS what for, Jack thought, seeing a pair of *Wildcats* strafing two of the Japanese destroyers attempting to approach *Johnston*'s battered hulk. There were at least four of the little tubby fighters trying to give the *Johnston*'s crew time to get the boats off.

"Sir, why aren't they shooting at us with their main guns?" the steward asked.

"What's your name, sailor?" Jack asked.

"Seaman 1st Class Doherty, sir," the man replied.

"Probably low on ammunition, Doherty," Jack replied. He suddenly felt cold, almost sluggish.

Shock, he thought. *I'm going into fucking shock. That or the morphine is kicking my ass harder than I realized.*

"Someone get those damn depth charges safed!" he heard a voice shouting. It sounded like Lieutenant Worling, the *Johnston*'s chief engineering officer.

Glad the black gang had some folks get out, Jack thought. *Most of the damage must be forward*. He could hear the distant rumble of the battleship's guns, but strangely could not draw up the energy to fear incoming fire.

That's weird, he thought. *Why am I not…*

Johnston whipsawed violently, a massive waterspout erupting from the stern. The only thing that kept the motion from flinging Jack over the side was Doherty's quick grip under his shoulders.

"Fucking torpedoes!" someone shouted, pointing to where Jack could not see. Then he saw the long, cigar-shaped motion of a weapon passing just off the *Johnston*'s starboard side.

"She's going under!" someone shouted. Doherty turned to look aft, cursed, then heaved Jack up over the side of the Carley float nearby. Rather than a sharp pain, Jack felt a dullish ache from his legs. Then suddenly the *Johnston* seemed to be falling away from the raft and Doherty, the destroyer rumbling as bulkheads gave way under the surface. The fifteen or so sailors around the raft all began kicking and swimming furiously, helped in their cause by a sudden outrushing of air from some compartment collapsing.

Strange, I always thought there'd be suction, Jack thought. He recognized the terrible wreckage that was the pilothouse flashing by, bodies and parts of sailors hanging from the wreckage before it blissfully slid out of sight.

I hope someone listened to Worling…

The thought was distant and amorphous, like mental cotton candy. After a minute or two passed without a rumbling explosion, Jack realized either the ash cans had been blown off when the battleship finally caught *Johnston* with her 14-inchers or had indeed been rigged safe.

"Holy shit!" someone shouted. "That big bitch is… *FUCKING YES! AGAIN!*"

THE STREAM OF PROFANITY WAS SOMEWHAT WARRANTED. Lieutenant Hargen had understandably misjudged *Haruna*'s speed, even with the aid of radar. Were it not for *Heermann*'s hit, the *Kongo*-class battleship would have just barely avoided all ten of *Johnston*'s tin fish. Instead, the five white wakes from the forward torpedo mount continued their inexorable path through desperate weapons' fire towards the battleship. For a brief moment, Fate continued the favor that had kept *Haruna* largely undamaged throughout the entire war. *Johnston*'s first hit, in an outcome that would have brought Lieutenant Hagen to great anger if he were still alive, struck the battleship just abaft her forward magazine…and failed to detonate.

Then, fickle as always, Fate immediately removed her favor. The second torpedo, running deep, impacted just underneath the battleship's massive pagoda bridge. The crew had just barely recovered from that impact when the next hit between her stacks. The third, and final weapon struck between the No. 3 and No. 4 turrets. *Haruna* staggered like a speared great beast, oil gushing from her opened port side to leave an ersatz blood trail. In minutes, the combination of spall, inrushing water, and venting steam killed every sailor in the port side engineering spaces. This maiming was compounded by electrical arcing through the battleship's central dynamo room as shock knocked the vessel's generators off their moorings. As momentum continued carrying her forward, the *Haruna* began sharply listing to port, smoke starting to pour from her amidships as the unrefined oil in her bunkerage caught fire.

Someone just needs to shoot that poor bastard crying for his mother, Jack thought. *I'm no medical expert, but I'm pretty sure he ain't going to make it.*

"Well at least they wasted a torpedo on us," someone muttered from beside Jack. He turned his head to see Lieutenant Worling resting with his back against the side of the Carley float. Before Jack could respond, Worling gave a soft sigh, then slumped with his eyes open. Jack levered up on his elbow, fear suddenly cutting through the morphine. It was only then he realized the officer's entire right side, previously hidden from his view, had been shredded by fragments.

"Goddammit," the corpsman who had stuck him earlier said, having come aft in the raft. He closed Worling's eyes, then looked over at Jack.

"Sir, you don't look so good," he said.

"To be honest," Jack croaked, "I don't feel so good."

"It looks like we may have gotten the bastards from all that smoke," the corpsman said as he got closer to Jack.

"Hey! Anyone else feel that?!" someone asked from beside the raft. "*Did anyone else fucking feel that?*"

"Just shut up and kick it if the damn thing comes back around," one of the other men holding onto the raft barked.

"I gotta get into the raft," the first man replied, his voice rising in tenor. Jack felt the Carley float shift.

"Sailor, if you don't fucking get ahold of yourself right now, you're not going to have to worry about the damn sharks!" the second man, clearly a chief petty officer, shouted. The first sailor must have stopped trying to get into the raft, as suddenly things were still once again. After a few more minutes, Jack realized he did not hear any more aircraft, but that the rumble of ship engines was near constant.

"Where are the Jap destroyers?" he rasped.

"What was that, sir?" the corpsman asked, clearly distracted by something happening in the distance.

"Where are the destroyers?" Jack managed again.

"They're sitting about a half mile away signaling with that cruiser, sir," the corpsman said. "It looks like we really did a number on that battleship. She's burning something fierce."

I'm suddenly not sure if we're safer in this raft or on those destroyers, he thought. *It's not like our own side will know there are prisoners onboard. Or care, for that matter.*

"Shit," the corpsman said so quietly that Jack was

probably the only person who heard him. The young sailor spoke up louder after swallowing. "It looks like they're coming in to start taking prisoners."

No, Jack thought. *I will not be taken prisoner by those people.*

Jack grabbed the rope behind him, trying to lever himself up. The pain that shot through Jack's legs at even that weak effort served full notice being a prisoner wasn't up to him. The sailors holding onto the Carley float, however, clearly felt differently. Men began shouting back and forth to one another as they kicked away from the raft, striking out at various speeds.

"Corpsman," Jack said, struggling to be heard in the din. "Corpsman!"

"Sir, just a sec…"

The deep staccato of a heavy machine gun stopped the conversation. One moment the corpsman had been looking at Jack. The next, two rounds had carried away most of the man's chest cavity in a spray of gore. The sailor was dead before his body hit the raft, even as the burst was walked forward into the clump of injured men towards the bow.

I gotta get out the raft.

Despite realizing his mortal danger, Jack could not find the motivation. The machine gun fire started to walk back towards him and he closed his eyes. The impact of bullets to his left side caused him to open his eyes again…just in time to see the rounds had missed him because the Japanese crew could not depress the gun far enough. The destroyer's bow loomed in front of him, a bow wave raising as the vessel continued to build up speed.

God please, help me…

Whether divine influence or simple physics, Jack was suddenly lifted up and away from the Carley float as the Japanese destroyer slammed into it. Then his world was a whirling kaleidoscope of images as he desperately tried to hold his breath and struggle towards the surface. First flashing silver as the sun's rays fell upon a massive hammerhead swimming by, struggling sailor in its jaws. Then the wreckage of the Carley raft, bobbing like a shattered toy as it was pushed around in the destroyer's wake. A splash drew his head back behind him just as he was reaching the surface. It took a moment for oxygen-starved brain to process that what he'd seen was a cylindrical object that looked just like many homes' "ash can" trash receptacles.

No...

The hammer blast from the depth charge snuffed Jack's life almost instantly. Many others of the *Johnston's* crew were not as fortunate, succumbing to their wounds in minutes rather than seconds. Mrs. Murphy's grief would be shared by two hundred and seventy other families, with only two men ever seeing the United States ever again.

THE MURDEROUS RETRIBUTION VISITED BY THE JAPANESE destroyermen upon their American counterparts was, in the end, only a brief opening to a coda of carnage. Even as the last depth charges were carrying out their deadly work, the *Haruna's* demise arrived swiftly. Subjected to far more underwater damage than her designers had ever intended, the battleship's strong hull still gave a brief illusion of hope to her master, Captain Shigenaga. Having given orders intended to slow the *Haruna's* seemingly inexorable list to port, Shigenaga was heartened as the battleship began to settle in the water and start to come back to starboard.

This optimism, however, swiftly turned to horror as the combined effect of the battleship's massive pagoda mast's momentum coupled with the "surface effect" of tens of thousands of tons of water sloshing in her compartments swiftly took over. In the horrified view of the *Yahagi* and the destroyers rushing to attend to the battleship, the *Haruna* slowly then with stunning swiftness began to list back to port.

On *Haruna*'s bridge, Captain Shigenaga and most of his companions did not even have time to stop their sharp, sudden trip across the structure. *Haruna*'s master had the terrible misfortune to land atop his helmsman, thus being spared blessed transition to unconsciousness. Instead, the poor man broke both of his legs, then suffered the indignity of having the Emperor's portrait landing upon his head. Stunned, Shigenaga rolled onto his back to see the inclinometer passing thirty-five degrees.

As gruesome as the jumble of screaming men, heavy equipment, and flying glass was in on the bridge, it at least happened in daylight. Belowdecks, many of the *Haruna*'s compartments had been reduced to complete darkness by the American torpedoes. As Newtonian physics and fluid dynamics did their terrible work, these spaces became mixing vats combining sharp edges, human beings and ordnance. In the No. 2 turret's main trunk, as the list swept past forty degrees, a 14-inch shell fell out of the lifting tray. The 1,485-lb. shell smashed through the hatch to the powder room, delivered the tender mercy of decapitating two ratings en route to the far bulkhead, then smashed into waiting propellant bags on the bulkhead wall.

Whether the result of the cordite in the bags igniting via compression, an errant spark as metal met metal, or the high explosive shell's own contents reacting poorly to jostling, the shell exploded. In less time than their brains could realize what was happening, every officer and rating in No. 2 turret died. Even worse for *Haruna*'s crew at large, the resultant conflagration rent overwhelmed the flash doors and continued downwards into the magazine. As flame met powder with predictable results, the No. 2 magazine detonated, followed almost immediately by the No. 1 and forward secondary magazines. The massive series of blasts, in addition to shearing off the off the battleship's forward section, abruptly ended Captain Shigenaga's service to his Emperor. The subsequent disappearance of the battleship's hulk in five minutes did the same for over one thousand of Shigenaga's subordinates.

IJNS YAMATO
0735 LOCAL

"SIR, THE *HARUNA* HAS BLOWN UP!"

There were gasps and hushed curses behind Ugaki at the runner's announcement. He brought his binoculars down to his chest, concentrating on maintaining his calm as Lieutenant Commander Ryuunosuke received the ensign runner's full report.

It would appear that the American destroyers have also fixed their torpedoes, Ugaki thought bitterly. *A wonderful development to match what we have learned about their aerial torpedoes over the last two days.*

Ugaki looked out the compartment window at the rest of his force. For a few brief, blissful moments it appeared that the American aircraft had been forced to return to their carriers to rearm and refuel. One group of those carriers was just over fifteen miles to the east, their shapes occasionally visible through the haze and squalls. Ugaki had forbade the Center Force from taking them under fire, the targets too fleeting in the diminishing visibility to justify expending ammunition.

Suddenly I am not sure this is the right choice, Ugaki mused.

"Sir…" Lieutenant Commander Ryuunosuke started.

"I heard," Ugaki said, turning to face his chief of staff.

Ryuunosuke nodded, started to open his mouth, then closed it.

"Speak," Ugaki said.

Unless you are going to say 'I told you so.' At which point I will kill you.

"Sir, we must deal with the carriers," Ryuunosuke said in a rush. "The attacks are incessant, and it is only dumb luck that the Americans only hit the *Haruna*."

Ugaki nodded, the motion causing Ryuunosuke's face to briefly show surprise before he regained his bearing.

"They are like nests of *osuzumebachi*," Ugaki said grimly. "If we allow them to continue to sting us, eventually we will be slowed and killed. What do you propose?"

Ryuunosuke thought for a moment.

"While we could catch them with the battleships, that is a waste of ammunition and time," the junior officer replied. "I recommend we detach Vice Admiral Kazutaka's division and half the remaining destroyers to take care of this second carrier group."

Ugaki looked on as Ryuunosuke pointed at the plot.

"The third we can get in passing as we head for the beaches. They are likely having to rearm their aircraft. If Kazutaka can force them to turn out of the wind, that should help."

It will be a long stern chase, Ugaki thought. *But I do not see what other choices we have.*

"Make the signal to the *Kumano*," he said. "Tell Kazutaka to concentrate on the carriers, let his destroyers handle the escorts."

Ugaki was about to continue when the same ensign who had reported the *Haruna*'s demise returned.

That young man will drop dead from exhaustion before this day is over, Ugaki thought, seeing the officer's red face. *It is unfortunate that the bomb hit destroyed the communications to the radio room.*

"Yes ensign?" he asked, gesturing for the officer to come over.

"Sir, Vice Admiral Fukudome reports that his aviators believe they have sighted the American carriers to the far south," the ensign huffed. "They are having trouble attacking through the clouds. The Special Attack Units will likely be attacking within the hour, however."

With how poorly his pilots are trained, they will be a bonus if they just keep those damned fighters too busy to strafe us, Ugaki thought grimly.

"Special Attack Units?" Ryuunosuke asked, perplexed.

"Divine Wind," Ugaki said. "The men who will hopefully help solve our hornet problem."

Ryuunosuke nodded, now understanding.

Today will truly be a day spoken of for generations, Ugaki thought. *Thousands of men, all sacrificing themselves for the good of our nation. The Americans may truly rethink how far they wish to push this by the time we are done.*

"Order the *Yahagi* to break off rescue operations immediately," Ugaki said. "We will need her guns."

THE TERRITORY OF SURPRISE

U.S.S. Natoma Bay (Banjo Base)
0750 Local

"And may this sailor rejoin us all when the sea gives up her dead…"

This day has gone from bad to worse, Aaron thought as the *Natoma Bay*'s chaplain finished the liturgy for the dead. The chaplain raised his voice, trying to compete with the passage of the wind down the escort carrier's flight deck. The rustling of the air was exacerbated by the pounding of rain on the carrier's wooden deck from the squall.

It was pure dumb fortune I landed on a ship with a Roman Catholic chaplain, Aaron thought, tears rolling down his cheeks in the rain. *It was the least I can do for Rizzo after killing him.*

The escort carrier's flight deck crew stood anxiously around his battered *Avenger*, nervously glancing towards the island then back towards the northwest.

"Hey buddy, they're going to need to clear the flight deck soon," the carrier's LSO said from beside him. The other lieutenant had come over from his platform.

I suspect someone from the bridge passed the word that we needed to hurry this up, Aaron thought. *They can wait thirty goddamn seconds.*

"Rizzo was a good crewman," Aaron snapped. "If you're not going to take the time to cut him out of the aircraft, I'll be damned if we're not going to give him a proper burial according to this faith."

The other officer gave Aaron an understanding look.

"I get it," he said. "I lost my tail gunner at Saipan."

The man pointed astern, where several of Taffy 2's escorts could be seen forming up.

"But apparently some Jap cruisers are starting to catch up with us, and we need to clear the flight deck so the CAP can land and get some refueling before we launch what *Avengers* we have left."

The LSO looked like he was about to say something else when he stopped and looked up at the *Avenger*. The man's face turned solemn as he made the sign of the cross.

"Amen," he shouted, along with several of the flight deck crew.

Aaron turned and watched as the chaplain, the service completed, began to crawl down off the *Avenger*'s wing. The man's vestments were flapping in the wind, the *Natoma Bay*'s engines audibly straining as she fled.

"Clear the flight deck," the island loudspeaker boomed. "I say again, clear the flight deck."

Guess that's that, Aaron thought bitterly, looking over as Radioman 1C Morgan leaned on a corpsman and hobbled to the flight deck's edge. Aaron moved to catch up with the duo, struggling against the wind. Just as he approached them, there was the sound of metal catching metal as the

Avenger caught the port side gallery deck before continuing over the side.

Goodbye Rizzo, Aaron thought as the dark blue aircraft came into sight astern. It was flat on its back, sinking rapidly.

"No, fuck that, I'm not going down into the ship," Morgan shouted.

"Look pal, you either go down to the galley and get some morphine or I sew you up right here," the corpsman snapped. "I think you'd rather have the surgeon do it."

"No, no, I'd rather stay here where I can get off this damn ship if those cruisers catch up with us," Morgan replied. Behind him, a petty officer was starting to step away from the 40mm guns.

"Sew him up here," Aaron said, stepping closer behind the corpsman.

"Who the hell asked…" the corpsman turned, stopping his question abruptly. "…uh, sir. That's not standard unless we're in action."

Aaron saw the petty officer returning to his gun.

"You're about to be in action," Aaron replied, his face grim. "Morgan and I saw firsthand what happens this morning when one of these ships gets hit by gunfire. If you're right, he gets to be in pain and have a terrible scar."

Aaron turned and looked astern just in time to see waterspouts landing around the destroyer on the horizon.

"On the other hand, if *we're* right, you can thank us when we're in the water and not burning to death below."

The corpsman swallowed, and Aaron had a moment's regret at his frankness.

Fuck it, I'm done sugar coating things, he thought. After a brief moment of contemplation the corpsman shrugged, got out a pair of scissors, and began cutting at Morgan's uniform.

"Hey sir," Morgan started, wincing as the scissors struggled with his wet uniform.

"Yes Morgan?" Aaron asked.

"I'm sorry about what I said up there," he said, then grunted as the corpsman pulled at ripped cloth. "Jesus buddy, I'm not a Honolulu mistress!"

"Look pal, you're the one who wanted to get sewn up here," the corpsman snapped. "You're bleeding all over the damn place and you're soaked. Hold still."

"Don't worry about it, Morgan," Aaron said. "You didn't say anything that wasn't true."

"Nothing you could've done, sir," Morgan said. "Those bastards just got lucky."

I could've left the last dummy run alone, Aaron silently disagreed. *Rizzo would still be alive if I had. Not sure crippling that Jap battleship made any difference anyway.*

The corpsman finished cutting away Morgan's uniform, then grabbed some forceps.

"Goddammit, can't you give me something before you start pulling shit?!" Morgan said, seeing the instrument out of the corner of his eye.

"No," the pharmacist mate replied. "Doc is saving all the morphine for people once we're hit."

You probably won't need it, Aaron thought bitterly. Recalling the conflagration that had been the *White Plains'* flight deck made his stomach do several flips, and he took a deep breath to stop from being sick.

"What the fuck is that idiot doing?" someone asked. Aaron looked up to see a sailor running from the carrier's island towards where Morgan and he stood. The man was slipping all over the place, and nearly fell to the deck as the *Natoma Bay* heeled over in a sharp turn to starboard.

That's not good, Aaron thought. *Why are we turning out of the wind?!*

"Air raid inbound! I say again, air raid inbound!"

Morgan shot him a worried glance, and Aaron hoped he did not look as terrified as his crewman did. The sailor, after sliding down the ladder to the gallery deck, made a beeline to where Aaron was standing.

"Sir, are you the pilot of that plane we just shoved over the side?" the sailor, looking not a day over sixteen, asked.

"No, he's the fucking tooth fairy!" Morgan muttered, and the young man recoiled as if Morgan had slapped him. Morgan jerked and swore as the corpsman pulled a fragment out of his back.

"I am," Aaron replied, shivering involuntarily as a trickle of water ran down his spine.

"The admiral would like to see you, sir," the sailor said. "Right now."

The 40mm gun briefly started to raise, then lowered as the crew began searching more intently over the side. Aaron heard engines in the clouds above them passing overhead.

"It would seem he's not really asking if it's 'right now,'" Aaron noted. He looked down the flight deck as *Natoma Bay* heeled over again, this time to port.

We're zigzagging, he thought. *Which if we're not launching immediately, makes some sense with enemy aircraft around.*

"Although if the captain keeps whipping the ship around like a destroyer, there's a good chance I'm gonna fall overboard off that flight deck," Aaron observed.

"Probably be easier if you went down the hangar deck!" the corpsman said, just as *Natoma Bay* reversed course again. The man was about to say something else when the gun talker looked up, ashen-faced.

"Holy shit, some Jap submarine just torpedoed the *Petrof Bay*!"

Aaron felt his stomach drop. The *Petrof Bay* was a

carrier in Taffy 1, the southernmost of the three 7th Fleet carrier groups.

Suddenly glad I told Rhodes to head for Tacloban, Aaron thought, shaken. *Apparently it's not safe out here from anything.*

"Sir, the admiral…" the sailor insisted. Aaron shook himself.

"Let's go," he said, gesturing.

THE CORPSMAN WAS RIGHT, AS PASSAGE TO THE FLIGHT deck was a relatively quick trip if one cut through the carrier's hangar deck. Aaron noted the beehive of activity as the *Natoma Bay*'s Airedales feverishly worked to rearm the four *Avengers* on the hangar deck. Aaron noted that the entire quartet had torpedoes next to them.

They've got to get the torpedo cradles into the bomb bays, he thought. *Christ that's going to take time we don't have with cruisers after us.*

"Sir, this way," the sailor said, bringing Aaron's attention back to him. Aaron found himself being ushered by a fellow lieutenant named Rackham into an *ad hoc* flag plot. Rear Admiral Felix Stump was tall and gangly, his face set grimly as he listened to his staff's reports.

"The *Haggard* is handing off fighter direction to the *Kadashan Bay*," a commander who Aaron assumed was the chief of staff stated. "Captain Reynolds has directed the *Oberrender* to continue making smoke. The rest of the DEs will stay with us."

"Thank you, Commander Pickering," Stump said, then turned towards Rackham.

"Who have you brought me, Rackham?" the admiral asked genially.

"Sir, Lieutenant…" the aide began, then stopped as he clearly had forgotten.

"Mackenzie, sir," Aaron said wearily. "From the *Gambier Bay*."

"Finally, someone from Taffy 3," Stump said, exasperated. "I can't get anyone to answer my radio calls and…"

"That's because they're probably mostly dead or fighting for their life," Aaron spat, interrupting. Hearing the shocked intake of breath, he realized he'd overstepped slightly. "Sir."

Stump nodded, waving off the breach in discipline.

"Son, you've had a rough day," the admiral said. "I'm sorry we made you sit up there in the pattern with your injured crew."

"Dead and injured, sir," Aaron corrected, then swallowed. "No matter, saw that you had to get the CAP off the deck."

Stump nodded, looking somewhat impressed at Aaron's quick assessment of the tactical situation as he continued.

"Last thing you needed was to end up with a hole in the ship if I pranged the landing. Rizzo wasn't getting any deader and my plane wasn't going to fly again."

Stump's eyes narrowed at that.

Yes, I'm probably teetering on the edge of shell shock, Aaron thought. *It's not like I've got a plane to fly anymore, and outside of divine intervention I'll have plenty of time to get over it when we're all in the water.*

"Tell me what happened from the beginning," Stump said, gesturing for one of his staff to hand Aaron a pointer. Taking the item, Aaron regarded the flag map and swallowed as he looked at the plot.

Those hostile vessels are a lot closer than I thought they were. Clearly they changed direction while I was in the pattern.

"Japanese jumped us this morning," Aaron began, pointing where Taffy 3's last known position was marked. It took him six minutes to give a quick, terse report. Aaron watched Stump's face grow progressively more concerned as he ran down everything through torpedoing the *Kongo*-class battleship. By the time he was done, the rear admiral's face was almost ashen, the rest of his staff similarly pale.

"So unless someone gets more airpower into the fight, biggest battleship you've ever seen is going to start laying waste to all of us," Aaron said. "I'm shocked it hasn't happened already."

"He seemed a lot more interested in getting past us than after us," Stump said, pointing at the plot. "Then something changed his mind."

Okay, maybe hitting that battleship was important. And we may have killed every man in this task force.

"You saw us get the CAP reinforced," Stump continued. "But it's starting to get crowded up there, especially down by Taffy One."

"Pretty sure the Japanese are throwing all their chips in, sir," Aaron said, thinking of the murderous flak and tracers once more. "Again, at least three battleships, possibly five. One is definitely crippled. We really need Third Fleet to show up."

"No one can get a hold of Third Fleet or that Task Force 34 they were supposedly forming," Stump said. "Vice Admiral Kinkaid has resorted to sending messages in the clear rather than routing them through MacArthur's headquarters. Stupid Army son of a bitch."

Stump gestured at his aide.

"Lieutenant Rackham suggested we make sure we get torpedo cradles into all the *Avengers*. I hope that doesn't get us all killed."

"Sir, quite frankly, 500-lb. bombs will bounce off them like BBs," Aaron said. "If we slow them down like we did that first one, maybe our battleships will get back from down south."

"Unlikely," Stump replied. "Although they'll at least get to the beach head in time to keep the Japanese from shooting up all the supplies, I suppose."

"Sir, if I may," Aaron said. "I suggest we try and coordinate with Taffy One. Part of what got people killed earlier was dribs and drabs."

"I'm talking with Rear Admiral Sprague," Stump said.

Who will probably be known as 'the one that survived' here shortly, Aaron thought as he winced. It had often been troublesome to figure out which Rear Admiral Sprague people were referencing, either Thomas for Taffy One or Clifton commanding Taffy Three. The Japanese had probably solved *that* problem permanently.

"Sir, we're already putting together orders with Taffy One's staff," Commander Pickering noted, scribbling furiously.

"Sir, report from Taffy One," a talker said from the commander's left. "The *Petrof Bay* is being abandoned."

"Goddammit," a lieutenant (j.g.) said, drawing a stern look from Stump.

No, no, he's right, Aaron thought, feeling sick to his stomach. *God has definitely damned the Navy today*.

"Sorry sir," the junior officer said. Stump nodded, then turned to look outside at the intensifying rain.

"We might have to launch the rest of our birds in this soup regardless," Stump stated. "I don't think we can outrun those cruisers for long."

"Sir, the *Haggard* and the other vessels are beginning torpedo runs," a talker reported. "There appear to be four Japanese cruisers and six destroyers coming right for us."

Before Stump could respond, a lieutenant commander appeared at the hatch. Like Aaron, he was in his flight suit.

"Sir, you wanted to see me?" the man asked.

"Disregard Lieutenant Commander Barnes," Stump

replied. "I was going to ask you to get two birds up to try and reach Taffy 3. However, Lieutenant Mackenzie tells me that won't be necessary."

Barnes looked at Aaron quizzically.

"He's from the *Gambier Bay*," Stump continued. "It appears that Third Fleet left the fence gate open and Taffy 3 got surprised this morning. That's why we haven't heard from them."

Barnes regarded Aaron with a speculative look.

Uh oh.

"Was that your bird I hear they shoved off the deck?" Barnes asked.

"Yes," Aaron said.

"Can you fly?" Barnes asked, looking him up and down.

Are you out of your fucking mind? Aaron thought, taking a deep breath. Before he answered, the *Natoma Bay*'s 1MC interrupted.

"Aircraft bearing oh one oh! All guns, all guns open fire!"

The din of the automatic weapons opening up made Aaron jump. No one else noticed in the compartment, several folks pointing forward at two dark green aircraft low on the water to their starboard bow.

Oh shit, they're coming in fast, Aaron thought. *They'll never drop torpedoes at that speed.*

As tracers begin spitting out towards the two aircraft, they split. One continued heading for the *Natoma Bay*, seeming to *accelerate*, much to Aaron's surprise. The second turned to port, turning its nose towards the escort carrier *Manila Bay*, astern of *Natoma Bay*.

"He can't drop a torp at that speed.." Barnes shouted, even as the *Natoma Bay* began heeling to port as she turned to starboard. The ship's bow was just coming past five degrees of turn when a 40mm round from the U.S.S. *Richard W. Suesens* blew its left wing off. Snap rolling towards the missing structure, the aircraft slammed into the ocean with a massive explosion.

"What the hell? He was carrying a bomb?!" Barnes observed, puzzled.

"Fish must have blown…" someone else started to shout from the back of the compartment.

Either one of them could be right, Aaron thought. *But unless he was going to skip it like the Army does, I don't see how he cou…*

The explosion behind and to their port side caused every man to turn and look. As he whipped around, Aaron saw the *Manila Bay*'s assailant explode in a ball of black smoke and fire. Then before him was a scene that made him nearly vomit and scream at the same time. The carrier *Ommaney Bay*, leading Taffy Two's second column, had been hit in her stern by *something*. The massive fireball looked suspiciously like the aftermath of an aircraft crash roiling upwards rather than a bomb hit.

"That bastard didn't even swerve!" one of Stump's staff said, his face pale. "He just came right up from astern, dropped his bombs, then…"

"*Oh shit! Another one!*"

Like a moth drawn to a flame, the second aircraft came racing in, trailed by a *Wildcat* with ships' tracers across its paths. The American fighter peeled off, drawing some friendly fire as the Japanese aircraft began a sharp climb. The single-engined aircraft then inverted.

There's no way he can pull off a loop that…

The arc terminated forward on the *Ommaney Bay*'s flight deck in a horrifying gout of flame followed closely by a bomb detonation. Portions of the wooden structure arced upwards with the blast, the boards fluttering across and astern of the stricken carrier. After a few seconds, there was a secondary explosion from the stern, then another forward.

Probably touched off some torpedoes if she was also preparing to launch a strike, Aaron thought, grabbing the plot table for support as his head started to swim. There were curses and yells from the men below as oily smoke began to belch from the hole on the bow. More explosions began from the stricken carrier's hangar deck, and Aaron could see men starting to jump off from the bow.

Combustible, vulnerable, and expendable, Aaron thought bitterly. *Certainly proving that true today.*

"Tell Captain Morehouse the radar plot needs to take over fighter direction," Commander Pickering barked, yelling to be heard over the ship's guns. The talker nodded, and Aaron listened as the man calmly began relaying instructions. The young sailor stopped midsentence, grasping his headphones tighter as he strained to listen. Starting in surprise, the sailor regained his bearing and waved Commander Pickering closer.

That has got to be very bad news, Aaron thought. He glanced astern and saw distant plumes of smoke starting to rise from where Taffy Two's escorts had been heading. *I suspect I know what it is.*

AARON WOULD HAVE DRAWN LITTLE COMFORT FROM knowing he was correct. Turned loose from their screening responsibilities, the commanders of the *Suzuya*, *Kumano*, *Tone*, *Chikuma*, and their accompanying destroyers reverted back to the IJN's default setting: violence of action. A veteran of the Solomons' combat, Vice Admiral Kazutaka strongly disagreed with Ugaki's directive for his cruisers to ignore the American destroyers. Having followed the radio traffic from the *Yahagi*, Kazutaka had absolutely zero desire to find himself abandoned to die in the warm waters off Samar.

For this reason, with a blinking signal light, Kazutaka gave orders distributing the four cruisers' fire as soon as the American light ships came into visual range. With higher numbers and heavier guns, the four Japanese heavy cruisers remained bow on to the U.S.S. *Haggard*, *Franks*, *Hailey*, and the destroyer escort *Abercrombie*.

Unlike the *Johnston*, the four American ships did not benefit from a near zero visibility squall to shield their movements. Although the driving rain did ensure the first the Japanese glimpse of the four vessels was at 17,000 yards, this was at extreme 5-inch range. The Japanese cruisers were well within their lethal envelope. Even with the Japanese crews' sharply reduced training due to fuel oil shortages and the threat of submarines, things could only go one way.

The *Franks* was the first American vessel hit. Just as the first aircraft were attacking the *Natoma Bay*, a pair of shells from the *Kumano* found the American destroyer's stern. In an eruption of steam, smoke, and screaming men, the destroyer's speed was cut in half. Realizing that his vessel was about to be shot out from under him, *Franks*' gunnery officer flung his torpedoes in a desperate salvo at slow setting. Only half the torpedoes were fired before *Kumano* made the correction and put a tight salvo of three shells in the *Franks*' superstructure. With her bridge crew dead and the gunnery director lost over the side, the *Franks*' executive officer belatedly attempted to take control. His first orders were received in the battered engineering spaces just in time for *Kumano*'s secondary guns to obliterate his position. It took barely three more minutes for the heavy cruiser to finish rendering the *Franks*' a burning, drifting wreck.

Haggard and *Hailey* only lasted a minute more than

their sister. For the former, two *Tone* 8-inch shells in the aft magazine caused an explosion that nearly severed the stern. Burning and without power, the *Haggard* was then riddled by 8 and 5-inch shells as the *Tone* continued to steam towards her. Two of the accompanying Japanese destroyers joined in as the range closed to 10,000 yards, peppering the American vessel with hits. Holed above and below the waterline, *Haggard* abruptly and violently capsized to starboard with most of her crew still at their posts.

Hailey, turning to port to avoid her sister's wreck, inadvertently corrected the bearing for a six-gun salvo from the *Suzuya*. Once more Japanese salvos' tight grouping wreaked havoc, as three hits and two near misses knocked out the *Hailey*'s power. Like *Haggard*, this meant *Hailey* was deluged by a storm of shells as the Japanese formation closed with her. Although not sinking as abruptly as *Haggard*, *Hailey*'s crew suffered mightily from the continued fire even as the destroyer began sinking stern first. Only as her bow rose out of the water towards the vertical did the *Suzuya* and the Japanese destroyers check fire. Unlike their brethren in DESRON 10, none of the Japanese vessels paused to shoot at the American survivors as they passed by.

"SIR, THE *OMMANEY BAY* REPORTS SHE'S LOST HER MAIN fire main," the talker continued, still straining to hear over the hammering AA fire..

Aaron looked up from the plot, watching as the stricken escort carrier started o drift astern of the main formation.

Captain turned her so her smoke would at least serve to screen the rest of us, Aaron noted. *I wonder if that was by design.*

"Signal her to abandon ship, my order," Stump said. "We can't stop to take off her survivors, best we can do is make sure they have plenty of time for an orderly evacuation."

Aaron heard Lieutenant Rackham take a deep breath. He turned to look at the other officer, whose face was now white as a sheet.

"Know someone aboard her?" he asked.

"My best friend Darryl," Rackham said, stricken. "Best man at my wedding."

Aaron nodded.

"I'm sorry," he replied.

"Lieutenant Mackenzie?" Barnes said from behind him, and Aaron turned. "I ask again, can you fly?"

Aaron felt several sets of eyes on him.

"At the moment, I've got a couple of ensigns rounding out my flight," Barnes continued. "One of whom, last I saw him, was busy puking into a bucket from fear."

Aaron met the man's gaze. Barnes didn't even bother looking ashamed at what he was asking.

You bastard, Aaron thought. *I've done enough for three men today, and you're basically bracing me to replace some yellow-bellied nugget rather than just kicking his ass.*

"I'm going to need a crew," Aaron replied, venom in his voice. "Seeing as mine got shot up helping to put a hole in a damn battleship."

"It's the ensign who is having a case of the nerves, not his gunner," Barnes replied evenly.

There was a low rumble that caused the flag bridge's windows to shake. Aaron looked astern in time to catch the last of the explosive fireball engulfing the *Ommaney Bay*'s stern. He closed his eyes and fought back nausea at the all too familiar sight.

Her magazine just went, he thought. *I might need that ensign to share his bucket.* Turning back to Barnes, he shrugged.

"Guess your ensign's going to be real shocked *when* that happens here," Aaron snapped. "Let's get to the hangar deck."

There was charged silence behind him as he headed for the hatch, but Aaron was far too angry to care if he'd offended anyone.

Damned if I fly, damned if I don't, he thought. *But I know for sure if I survive this fucking torpedo run I'm heading for Tacloban.*

USS WASHINGTON
0815 LOCAL

ORRICK LOOKED AT THE FLAG PLOT AND WILLED THE U.S.S. *Alaska* and her cohorts to close *faster* with the enemy.

Taffy 3 is down to a single sinking carrier and a couple of destroyer escorts fleeing for their life, he thought. *Taffy 2 is apparently being engaged by enemy aircraft that sound suspiciously like suicide bombers and, thanks to the submarines, Taffy 1 is down one carrier and is also under sustained attack from aircraft.*

Orrick shook his head.

"Something on your mind, Deuce?" Commodore Jeter asked from a few feet away, startling him. Orrick looked at him from down the plot.

"Just thinking that the postmortem for today is going to be very interesting," he observed. He took a deep breath. "Folks are going to wonder if we should have broken radio silence just to save those unfortunate fellows in Seventh Fleet."

"Vice Admiral Kinkaid has plenty of fighting power to remedy the situation," Jeter replied, tapping his hands angrily on the plot.. "The fact he's apparently let all his battlewagons go on a joy ride down in Surigao Strait is not this force's problem."

I somehow doubt Admiral Nimitz is going to see it the same way, much less Admiral King, Orrick thought, looking back down. *I mean, Jeter's right: Kinkaid's a dumbass. Seventh Fleet should never been allowed to basically become MacArthur's private navy for this op.*

"We have a chance to bag the entire Japanese battle line," Jeter continued. "They're now so far south in the Philippine Sea they can't get out if we plan this right.

Jeter gestured towards the north half of the plot.

"If the carriers don't get away from Vice Admiral Halsey, we might basically end the war *today*."

Everything you say is accurate, Orrick thought. *But it doesn't change the fact there's probably more dead sailors in the water right now than we lost at Pearl Harbor.*

"Sir, plain text communication from Pearl Harbor," a runner interrupted their conversation.

Speaking of Admiral Nimitz.

The young sailor patiently stood at parade rest at the other end of the command plot as Commodore Jeter made his way over to take the form.

"Did someone go to get Vice Admiral Lee?" Jeter asked as he maneuvered around the table.

"Yes sir," a chief petty officer answered. "The surgeon is with him right now."

"Sir, Rear Admiral DuBose reports he is within range of three small targets," a talker called out. "He requests permission to engage."

There was a sudden hushed silence in the flag plot.

*If DuBose broke radio silence to make that report, he clearly wants to engage **and** thinks the Japanese are about to sight him anyway.*

"Deuce, what's the likely reaction once DuBose opens

fire?" Jeter asked, glancing up from the message flimsy again..

Orrick looked down at the map.

"If he opens fire with his cruisers? That group of enemy cruisers chasing Taffy Two is going to keep after the carriers."

Orrick grabbed a pointer.

"On the other hand, if whatever vessels start screaming about battleships because the *Alaska* opens up?" Orrick said, pointing towards the northernmost contacts on the plot. "Well, I suspect that at the very least the cruisers are going to turn back north, if not the whole fleet."

"Looks like we'll have a chance to split the baby," Jeter said, then turned to address the talker. "Inform Admiral DuBose he may fire when ready."

"Aye aye, sir," the talker replied.

There goes radio silence, but at this point it doesn't matter.

Jeter looked around the compartment at the bustling staff.

"If anyone needs to use the head, I suggest you go do it now," he stated. "It's about to be your last chance."

Literally last chance if this goes poorly for us, Orrick thought. He shuffled over to where Jeter was starting to read the communiqué.

"Sir, you may want to remind Rear Admiral DuBose his role is to be more Hipper than Callahan," he stated. "The last thing we want is him taking on five Japanese battleships by himself."

"That son of a bitch," Jeter suddenly muttered, startling Orrick.

"Uh…" Orrick started.

"Read this," Jeter replied, shoving the message at Orrick, hands shaking.

Okay, I don't think he heard a word I said, Orrick thought, taking the message. He read it. *Oh.*

TURKEY TROTS TO WATER. GG FROM CINPAC ACTION THIRD FLEET INFO COMINCH CTF SEVENTY SEVEN GG WHERE REPEAT WHERE IS TF 34. RR THE WORLD WONDERS.

Okay, some comms officer at Pearl Harbor needs shot, Orrick thought. *Or maybe one in our comms shop for not requesting message confirmation.*

"It's padding," Orric said, handing it back. "Someone should have asked for confirmation to give Pearl a chance to fix it."

"What?"

"'The World Wonders' is padding," Orrick stated. "The comms officer at Pearl should have picked a different phrase to add as gibberish at the end of the message. They would have caught the error if they'd been asked to resend."

Orrick shrugged.

"I doubt anyone will remember what that message said in a year."

Jeter looked at him not understanding, then glanced past him and straightened up.

"Attention in the…" Jeter began, coming to attention.

"Carry on!" Vice Admiral Lee said, moving towards the table. "Commodore Jeter, a word. You too, Orrick."

"Yes sir," Jeter said, moving over to where the Vice Admiral was standing. Orrick followed a moment later.

That does not look like a man who may have been having a heart attack a little over an hour ago, Orrick thought, confused. *Maybe it was something else and I overreacted.*

"Commodore Jeter, while I appreciate the initiative,

command should have shifted to Rear Admiral Davis aboard the *Massachusetts*," Lee stated lowly so that only Orrick and Jeter could hear.

"Sir, I did not want to break radio silence to send the signal," Jeter replied.

"I understand," Lee replied, then looked over the map while continuing in a much more conciliatory tone. "Which is why I'm merely admonishing you, not having you locked in the brig."

His tone implies he's joking, but even I can sense that's not totally a joke, Orrick thought. From Jeter's expression, the commodore also got the implied message as Lee continued.

"Should I become incapacitated in the upcoming battle you must immediately pass word for Rear Admiral Davis to take command."

"Understood, sir," Jeter said.

"Rear Admiral Dubose is almost in contact, I assume?" Lee asked.

"Yes sir, he asked permission to fire," Jeter said. "I granted it to him."

Lee nodded, then gestured at the paper in Orrick's hand.

"Let me see that message," he stated.

Oh God, I hope he really hasn't had a heart attack, Orrick thought as he started to hand the message over.

"I suspect that someone made a mistake in padding at Pearl, sir," Orrick stated as the vice admiral took the paper. Lee raised his eyebrows, then he read the message.

I would never want to play poker with that man, Orrick thought, watching Lee's eyes pass over the message twice.

"A mistake in padding indeed," Lee replied, then smiled. "I think we'll make one of our own."

With that, Vice Admiral Lee gestured for a runner to

come over. As the sailor began making his way across the compartment, Lee took a pen out of his pocket. He scribbled something on the back of the message, reread it, nodded, then passed it to Orrick.

"You've barely had time to ever see me write anything while on the staff," Lee said. "So if you can read it, the comms shop should be able to also."

Why do I get the feeling I'm about to go down in history in the same way Beatty's signal lieutenant has? Orrick thought, taking the paper. He looked down at the message.

KENTUCKY WIND CLEARS SMOKE WL COMM TF 34 TO COMINCH PACFLT. ENGAGING ENEMY AT THIS TIME. WISH YOU WERE HERE. BH WONDER NO MORE

Orrick couldn't hold back his laugh.

Those are some very, um, interesting padding initials, he thought. *Nimitz will surely recognize Willis Lee and Bill Halsey. So much for messages no one will remember in 12 months.*

"Sir, I think that will definitely get some attention at Pearl," he said, handing the note back to Vice Admiral Lee. "Might make for an interesting conversation in a few days."

"In 'a few days' we'll either be dead," Lee replied, "or the men who broke the Japanese battle fleet. In either case, I don't think anyone will be court martialing me."

I wish I had half his confidence about the latter, Orrick thought. *But in either case, the die is cast*.

"Commodore Jeter, you go make sure this gets sent exactly as I've written it," Lee said. "I suspect the lack of contact from Vice Admiral Halsey means the *Santa Fe*'s seaplane has reached Third Fleet and at least *he* knows where I'm at."

"Yes sir," Jeter said.

"I took a step outside before I came back in here," Lee said. "Visibility seems to be getting better even if there are still a lot of squalls. I would have preferred for the rain to stay, as it would help blind the Japanese."

"Agreed, sir," Jeter replied. "When the time comes, what range do you wish to engage the enemy if the squalls do hold up."

"Well, much as I'd like to sneak up and club their asses like we did back in '42," Lee replied with a smile, "I guess 20,000 yards is reasonable."

"Aye aye, I will have the word passed," Jeter said. He looked over at Orrick.

"Deuce, you have anything to add?"

"Sir, from what is getting reported to higher, the escort carriers think they bagged a *Kongo*-class," Orrick replied. "That means we're going to have one of that new monster class, a pair of *Nagato*, and a *Kongo* to fight. I expect they'll turn to close the range with us inside of 20,000 yards. With the *South Dakota* having engineering problems, we may have trouble keeping them from doing so with the speed difference."

Lee considered what Orrick had said for a few moments, lost in thought. Nodding to himself, he turned to look at Jeter.

"We'll come up with a battle plan once you return from making sure that message gets to Admiral Nimitz," Lee replied. "I'm thinking we'll release the destroyers for a torpedo attack and expect the cruisers to keep their escorts off of us. See if the small boys can make this as unfair a fight as last night was for Oldendorff."

That was at night, Orrick thought. *The Japanese don't have good radar.*

Jeter looked apprehensive at that statement.

"Sir, I think we can outgun them even with even odds," Jeter said. "Deuce, correct me if I'm wrong, but a *Kongo* can't penetrate our armor at 20,000 yards, can it?"

"If ONI is right about their guns, no," Orrick replied. "While any of our *South Dakotas* or the *Washington* should make swiss cheese of her."

"The *Nagato*s are a bit more of a problem," Jeter continued, nodding. "But I trust our guns with the super heavy shells against either their belt or their decks. So unless that new battleship has a very good 16-inch gun, we should be fine."

"Wishing now we'd brought *Iowa* or *New Jersey*," Lee muttered.

"I think Admiral Halsey would have walked across the water to kill you himself if he'd woken up to *New Jersey* heading south and the carriers going north, sir," Jeter said. "Plus those two hermaphrodites are still with the Japanese carriers. Even if they are ancient, they'd kill our cruisers then the flattops if they somehow got within range."

Things must have been really desperate for the Japanese to put half a carrier deck on those two battleships, Orrick thought. *Doesn't matter, Jeter's right, we had to leave both* **Iowa**-*class.*

"Get that message sent and hurry back," Lee stated. "If Rear Admiral DuBose is making contact, we don't have much time."

IJNS Yamato
0825 Local

The terrible thing about a tail chase, Ugaki thought as he gazed at the *Yamato*'s flag plot, *is that they take forever, even when the enemy ships are slower.*

"Sir, Vice Admiral Kazutaka reports he is taking the

enemy carriers under fire," Ryuunosuke reported, message flimsy in his hand. "They report the Special Attack Unit aircraft managed to sink one of the enemy vessels. The carriers are apparently launching aircraft."

Ugaki nodded.

"It would appear that they are able to refuel and rearm their aircraft faster than we realized," Ugaki observed, rubbing his chin. "It is good that we decided to go after both groups. Speaking of which, how long until we are in range of the third American carrier group?"

"With the weather clearing, we expect to be in range in five minutes," Ryuunosuke stated. "Less if it continues to clear to our south as it has been doing for the last half hour."

"Sir, the *Haguro* reports she sees an enemy aircraft carrier burning."

Ugaki looked over at the man, recognizing him as the ensign who had been making all of the previous reports from the radio room.

"Ensign, what is your name?" he asked.

"Saito, sir," the ensign said, coming to attention.

"Ensign Saito, you have done good work today," Ugaki said. "Are there no other officers in the radio flat?"

"Sir, we have had to send several of the staff to replace personnel on the guns," Saito replied.

The American fighters may not be able to do damage to the hull, but the same cannot be said for the sailors, Ugaki thought. *Fatigue will become a problem if those carriers manage to get too many more attacks in.*

"Carry…"

One of Saito's remaining comrades burst into the flat, the petty officer looking as though someone had just been struck by lightning right in front of him.

This cannot be good news, Ugaki thought, right before the man began speaking.

"Sir, the *Yahagi* reports she is being engaged by an enemy battleship!" the man reported, and Ugaki fought to keep the shock off of his face.

"A battleship?" he asked, fighting to keep his voice level. "A singular battleship?"

"Yes, sir," the runner said, bringing him the message. Ugaki quickly read it.

One battleship, engaging from beyond visual range, he thought. *Hit and destroyed the* **Kiyoshimo** *with her second salvo. Enemy cruisers also involved.*

Ugaki felt bile rising in his stomach.

In a battle that has seen my superior's initial flagship sunk out from under him by submarine, then he and most of his staff killed by a bomb, I can now say this is the strongest surprise to date. Is this how Kimmel felt all those months ago?

"Sir, are you all right?" Ryuunosuke asked. Ugaki realized he had been staring at the message for several moments. Standing erect, he forced doubt from his mind.

"It would appear that Vice Admiral Ozawa's sacrifice is not as thorough as we had hoped," Ugaki stated, handing the message over. The younger officer read it, his hands trembling halfway through. Ugaki watched as the man quelled his tremors, then looked with a resolute expression.

Like me, he realizes that we have likely just read our death warrants, Ugaki thought. *The Americans will be between us and San Bernadino Strait even if we turned around right now.*

"Sir," Ryuunosuke's voice was quiet, "what are we going to do?"

Ugaki considered his response for a few moments, the tension in the compartment thickening with every heartbeat.

"We must continue to harry these smaller carriers," he said. "At least for now. Signal Rear Admiral Kimura to retreat towards us at his best speed. Direct Vice Admiral Kazutaka that he is to finish the carriers with his guns only and to save his torpedoes for the incoming heavy units."

"Yes, admiral," Ensign Saito replied. He repeated the orders to Ugaki for insurance sake. Upon receiving a nod, Saito bowed and rushed back down towards the radio flat.

"This system will not work once we enter into action," Ryuunosuke stated.

"I suspect that once we are in action it will all become superfluous," Ugaki said grimly. "If that is Halsey, we will be seeing his aircraft soon. Especially as this weather clears."

To Ugaki's surprise, the *Yamato*'s firing gong began to sound. He and Ryuunosuke shared a look just before the battleship shook as she fired her main guns. Ugaki strode to the front of the flag bridge, raising his binoculars. The battleship's massive turrets were off her port bow. Raising his binoculars, Ugaki could see a large plume of smoke on the distant horizon.

We appear to have closed the range to the last carrier group, he thought *The gods simultaneously smile upon and curse us with the clouds clearing quicker than I expected.*

THE *YAMATO* HAD INDEED MANAGED TO CLOSE WITH TAFFY 1. Or more accurately Mother Nature had withdrawn her protective cloak from Rear Admiral Sprague's battered force. Like every other escort carrier that had been hit that terrible morning, the torpedoed *Petrof Bay* had become an obvious loss within minutes. However, unlike Rear Admiral Stump, Rear Admiral Sprague had refused to abandon the crippled vessel's crew to their fate. In addition, Sprague was compelled to keep the offending Japanese submarine well below periscope depth while the surviving carriers fled southeastward.

This was how the destroyer escorts *Coolbaugh* and *Edmonds* found themselves revealed to the *Yamato*. Task saturated with rescuing survivors while also hunting for the elusive *I-26*, both vessels had failed to realize the rapidly clearing weather conditions. At a range of 19,000 yards, the *Coolbaugh* was fortunate that the *Yamato*'s first four-shell salvo was short by two hundred yards. Of more immediate concern was the charging light cruiser *Noshiro*. Sister ship to the *Yahagi*, the *Noshiro* possessed a slightly more experienced crew. This was displayed as the light cruiser straddled the *Coolbaugh* with her second main battery salvo, then immediately disabled the *Coolbaugh*'s rudder with her 76-mm secondaries. Lamed, the destroyer escort still attempted to turn her bow around via steering with her engines, hoping to buy the *Edmonds* time by engaging the *Noshiro* with her paltry 3-inch main battery. The uneven contest was preemptively ended before it began by *Yamato*'s next salvo as a single 18-inch high explosive round broke the destroyer escort's back.

Edmonds, partially shielded by the burning *Petrof Bay*, heard her companion's cries of alarm over the Talk Between Ships (TBS). Her commander, Lieutenant Commander Burrows, made an immediate decision to flee even before the *Coolbaugh*'s master urged her to do so. Even with the *Petrof Bay*'s hulk and extensive smoke providing some degree of concealment, the wise choice bought Burrows and his command a mere ten more minutes of life. *Noshiro*, after pumping six broadsides of 6-inch fire into the *Coolbaugh*'s drifting hulk, sighted the fleeing *Edmonds* at a range of 12,000 yards.

Despite Burrow's expert ship handling, the issue was

never in doubt. On the credit side of the ledger, the *Edmonds* scored three hits with her rapidly firing 5-inch guns as she flitted around like a water bug. Her three torpedoes, even launched at a bad angle, were a threat that caused the *Noshiro* to radically change course. Spurred by one of the accompanying destroyers of DESRON 2 asking if their flagship needed assistance, the *Noshiro*'s gunnery officer hit the *Edmonds* with the light cruiser's eighth salvo. The four 6-inch shells annihilated the bridge, the forward 5-inch mount, and the DE's galley. In addition to killing Burrows and dozens of *Petrof Bay*'s survivors, the explosions caused a blaze to start in the mount's ready ammunition.

Burning, circling, and out of control, the *Edmonds* was easy prey for the light cruiser's next broadside. The tightly grouped nine shells were as ruthless and efficient as an executioner's sword, igniting the destroyer escort's bunkerage, smashing her power plant, opening her hull, and starting a fire in her forward magazine. A bare five minutes later, even as her aft gun continued to fire and her scuppers ran red with blood, the *Edmonds*' suffered a series of secondary explosions that obscured her from the *Noshiro*'s fire. When the smoke cleared, the destroyer escort was gone, with a small gaggle of *Petrof Bay* and her own crew fighting to stay afloat in a spreading oil slick. Unlike the murderous DESRON 10, *Noshiro* and her surging companions did not stop to commit additional homicide.

UGAKI DROPPED HIS BINOCULARS AND ALLOWED HIMSELF A small, contented smile.

Fifteen minutes to kill both of those small ships, he thought. *In another thirty we will likely have destroyed the carriers they were escor…*

"Sir! The *Kongo* is under fire!"

Ugaki whirled around at the report.

"*What?!*" he asked, running towards the flag bridge's port wing. He was able to look aft just as two more ominously large waterspouts appeared just astern of the *Kongo*. Ugaki felt his stomach clench, bile in his throat.

My God, the Americans are upon us...

"How did we let the Americans get within visual range without anyone telling me?!" Ugaki shouted, the words coming out in a rush.

Screaming at the staff will do you no good.

"Sir, there are no reports of the Americans within visual range!" Ryuunosuke replied, his own eyes darting wildly across the plot. "Our last report was from the *Yahagi* two minutes ago reporting that American cruisers had closed the range to 12,000 yards and she was engaging with torpedoes."

Once more, waterspouts rose around the *Kongo*. This time there were four of them, and they were almost certainly close enough that splinters had hit the vessel. Ugaki brought up his binoculars and watched as *Kongo*'s captain began evasive maneuvers. The smaller battleship began to fall back from *Yamato* as the maneuvers caused her to lose speed.

*Watching the **Kongo** chase salvoes accomplishes nothing!* Ugaki fumed. Dropping his binoculars, he moved quickly to his flag plot.

"If the Americans are firing on the *Yahagi*, which they were fifteen minutes ago, *who* is firing on the the *Kongo*?!" he asked.

"We do not know, sir!" Ryuunosuke replied.

.   .   .

Vice Admiral Ugaki would have been shocked to know the answer was the U.S.S. *Alaska*. His shock would have become *deep concern* had he known the "large cruiser" was more "lobbing shells to get a Japanese admiral's attention" than actually attempting to hit the *Kongo*. Rear Admiral DuBose, despite Commander Jeter's concerns, was well aware that his role was to entice Center Force north rather than become decisively engaged.

The initial gambit DuBose had chosen was to fire upon the *Yahagi* and her consorts. All this had accomplished was the *Yahagi* and the surviving destroyers fleeing due east, *away* from the rest of Center Force which was going due south. After belatedly recognizing Rear Admiral Kimura's brave attempt at self-sacrifice (if ignorant of the concurrent insubordination), Rear Admiral DuBose had split his force into three parts. The first consisted of the *Alaska* and a quartet of destroyers that would continue the pursuit of Vice Admiral Ugaki at flank speed. Next were the cruisers *Miami*, *Biloxi* and *Mobile* and four destroyers, under the command of Rear Admiral Joy, with their objective the destruction of the *Yahagi* and DESRON 10. Finally, DuBose himself rushed to the southeast with the cruisers *New Orleans*, *Wichita*, *Santa Fe*, and *Vincennes* accompanied by his remaining four destroyers. Although no particular force had superiority over their Japanese counterparts, DuBose's intent was simply to stop the CVE's destruction until Vice Admiral Lee could come up with his four battleships.

Thus had the *Alaska*, with her brand new Mark 13 gunnery radar, found herself chasing four Japanese battleships at just over 35,000 yards. What ensued was twenty-five agonizing minutes of generating a fire control solution, ensuring that the *Alaska* was not about to commit fratricide, and then closing another 5,000 yards. Throughout this, neither American nor Japanese eyes had seen the *Alaska* and her quartet of protectors. America's largest cruiser, named for the nation's newest territory, had achieved total and complete surprise when she'd opened fire.

WHAT HAS HAPPENED HERE? Ugaki THOUGHT ANGRILY, looking at the confused plot. *How did we lose track of an American battleship?!*

"Sir, the *Yahagi* reports DESRON 10 has launched all their torpedoes," Ryuunosuke said somberly. "She is coming about to engage the enemy more closely in the hopes that her sacrifice will buy us time to finish the mission."

"What do you mean, coming about?" Ugaki asked flatly, staring despondently at the plot. "She was ordered to rejoin us!"

Ryuunosuke shrugged helplessly.

Damn the Americans and their radar, Ugaki thought. *I am so* **blind**.

"Sir, the *Noshiro* has sighted the enemy carriers!"

Finally, he thought. *Perhaps we can at least cripple this southern group so that they cannot launch aircraft...*

"Signal from the *Kongo*! She has been hit by a shell that did not explode."

Ugaki exhaled, his breath almost whistling from frustration.

I am torn between killing the enemies before me or turning to destroy this single foe, Ugaki thought. *But if we allow that single American to continue to fire without punishment, we will be doomed. Especially at this range.*

"Sir..." Ryuunosuke began, concern in his voice.

"I know," Ugaki replied. "The Americans have spent decades preparing to engage us at long range. If this is one of their damned fast battleships with the 16-inch guns, they will cut *Kongo* to ribbons."

*Hell, even **Nagato** and **Mutsu** are at risk,* he thought. *The irony of the latter being repaired just in time to die without being able to fire a shot in her own defense would be overwhelming.*

"Bring us about," Ugaki said. "All vessels will turn after *Yamato*. If they want to pepper us at long range, I will at least have a vessel that can take the abuse in the lead."

"Yes sir," Ryuunosuke replied, bowing. "I will deliver the message myself."

The Emperor is lucky to have men such as him, Ugaki thought. *I have just informed him that we will be drawing the enemy's fire. Yet he simply returns to his duty without a second's hesitation.*

Ugaki looked around the flag plot as his remaining staff tended to their jobs.

Fine men, all of them, he thought. *It is a privilege to lead them to their deaths. I can only hope we will destroy enough of the Americans that they will reconsider seeking this 'unconditional surrender' they have spoken of.*

Ugaki felt the *Yamato* began to shift under his feet. As the mighty battleship began her turn, he realized he'd forgotten something.

"Have the *Noshiro* break off her pursuit," Ugaki stated. "Send plain text for Admiral Fukuodome to please concentrate his aerial attacks on the southernmost group."

His staff acknowledged, turning to their tasks. Ugaki gazed out the port bridge wing as the *Yamato* completed her turn onto a reciprocal heading to the rest of the battleline. First *Nagato*, then *Mutsu* passed his field of view, their turrets swinging as their gunnery officers scanned for targets that were far beyond sight.

Even with the lessening clouds, we would have to be very lucky to see either of the American carrier groups, Ugaki thought. *Although Kazutaka was surely within range of the carriers he was pursuing.*

"Sir, we have crippled another enemy carrier!" Saito stated from the compartment hatchway. "Rear Admiral Kazutaka asks if you wish for him to continue pursuit or rejoin the battle line?"

Ugaki considered his subordinate's question for a long minute before he heard the distant sound of incoming shells. Seconds later, a quartet of American shells landed a few hundred yards astern and to port of *Kongo*.

At least their accuracy is falling off, he thought. *That or they are getting our signal confused with* **Kongo***'s.*

Ugaki was not quite sure how radar worked. The sets mounted on the *Yamato* were temperamental and prone to inaccurate returns when searching for hostile ships. Still, they had helped his force find the Americans that morning, so he knew the electronics were usually sound.

They cannot seem to find this damned American battleship, he thought angrily. *Or at least, not at a range that is helpful.*

"Sir! *Haguro* reports she has a large radar contact!" Saito said, heading for the map as he came back into the compartment. Ugaki and Ryuunosuke met the younger officer at the plot, the staff parting as the young came through

"The contacts are…"

The increased of ripping canvas triggered an instinctual crouching response the experienced officers in the room. For his part, Ugaki did not stir, trying to figure out the fight's geometry in his head.

The enemy must be in three separate groups, he thought, noting that the *Yamato* had not been hit. *They have split their forces to get us to stop hurting the small carriers. Just as I split to pursue them.*

Ugaki spared a moment to look forward out of the

bridge's shattered windows. The weather was continuing to improve to the north and east, and he noticed the *Yamato*'s turrets pointed hopefully in that direction.

"Issue the order that none of the battleships are to fire on enemy carriers," Ugaki said. "We must save our ammunition for the enemy battleships when we sight them."

Ryuunosuke nodded, turning to direct a younger staff member to pass the message. The junior lieutenant nodded and moved quickly to head down to the radio room. Saito, for his part, had finished plotting the *Haguro*'s radar contact.

"The enemy vessel is 30,000 yards away and closing rapidly," Ryuunosuke noted. "Do you think he realizes we've come about?"

"I am sure he will figure it out fairly quickly," Ugaki replied, his voice flat. "The damnable American electronics work much better than ours."

To be able to see in the darkness, Ugaki thought. *In the fog. On a morning like this when it seems even the gods are taking the side of our enemy.*

Ugaki strode back once again to the flag bridge's windows. The wind rustling through the shattered windows was warm on his face, the smell of the sea air familiar even with the faint, lingering smell of gunpowder from the *Yamato*'s anti-aircraft guns. He looked to the northeast, towards far off Japan.

Oh Tomoko, I shall join you today, he thought. *The Americans have trapped us here, and I can only hope to do unto them all the harm that I can.*

Ugaki took a deep breath, closing his eyes at the thought of his late wife. He heard rapidly approaching footsteps from behind him and snapped them back open. Wearily, Ugaki turned around.

"Sir," Ryuunosuke said, his face pale. "Admiral Kazutaka reports four large contacts on radar to his north. They are closing at twenty-five knots, range 30,000 yards from his position."

So, the American battle line has arrived, Ugaki thought.

"The initial American battleship?"

"Has turned around and is moving away from us at thirty knots," Ryuunosuke replied, his tone incredulous.

"Confirm that report," Ugaki said. Ryuunosuke gave a slight bow.

"I already have, sir," he replied somberly. "It would appear to be one of the newer American vessels, an *Iowa*-class."

Was Halsey's reported move north all a feint? Ugaki wondered, aghast. *It's the only answer that makes sense. There are no other American battleships that fast.*

Ugaki could feel himself starting to panic. As he was about to speak, his hand brushed the sword at his side. Like oil on a tempestuous sea, the weapon helped him to center his raging psyche.

I have the finest battleship Japan has ever made, he thought. *Two full squadrons of destroyers and cruisers still with their torpedoes. If the Americans wish to trap us like they did the Southern Force, we will show them that these vessels are stronger than Nishimura's could dream of being.*

BUSHIDO IS NAILED TO THE MAST

USS WASHINGTON
0855 LOCAL

"SIR, unknown large contacts are on radar, relative bearing oh seven oh, range 30,000 yards," a talker's voice broke through the tense silence in flag plot. "Speed twenty-four knots."

Finally, Orrick thought, looking up from the plot. *Finally we can see the bastards.*

"Reconfirm with Rear Admiral DuBose the contact bearing oh seven six at 19,000 yards is the *Alaska,*" Lee said quietly from where he stood by the plot. "Destroyers are to remain in the screen."

"Aye aye, sir," Jeter replied. "What do you want the *Alaska* to do when she stops running?"

"She can maneuver independently in support of the battle line and await further orders," Lee said. "I don't want her to come about and end up with a torpedo or two for her trouble, and it sounds like the Japanese big ships can't quite clearly see her yet."

Future professors at Newport are not going to be happy with either Lee's decisions or the plot's inaccuracy to this point, Orrick thought, looking at the map. From the *Washington*, the contact that was likely *Alaska* and her four destroyer escort were off the starboard bow at roughly ten miles. The large cruiser was still not visible to the *Washington*'s lookouts, hence Lee's hesitation.

Although, outside of the **Kongo***-class, no Japanese battleship is moving that fast,* Orrick realized. *Shit. Should have said something to that effect.*

To the *Washington*'s port bow, Rear Admiral DuBose's cruisers had been visible for several minutes, even if what they were falling back from was not. According to the talkers, the *Wichita* had been hit in the engine room by a Japanese battleship's shell. The heavy cruiser had been lamed, meaning the Japanese task force as a whole had started closing the range.

DuBose had better get a Medal of Honor out of this, Orrick thought. *I cannot imagine being on a cruiser with a battleship shooting at me. I'd simply run and keep running.*

"I just hope they don't hit the *New Orleans* again," Jeter muttered.

The *New Orleans*, DuBose's only other heavy cruiser, had subsequently taken three shells from her Japanese counterparts. Built to the prewar Washington Treaty limits of 10,000 tons, the *New Orleans'* armor had been far too thin to keep the hits from penetrating her deck. A large fire had started in her aircraft hangar and, combined with another in her No. 3 turret handling room, had forced her crew to flood the aft magazines.

"They're going to keep hitting her until they can hit us, unfortunately," Orrick replied. He saw Vice Admiral Lee take a long drag on a cigarette at his statement.

Our plan to just stand off at radar and pound them to bits has fallen apart, Orrick thought. *A harder man might have simply let the Japanese maul DuBose as our four battleships shot them to pieces from relative safety, then cleaned up all their light vessels.*

He glanced over at Vice Admiral Lee as the commander studied the map. The Kentuckian showed no signs of his earlier medical episode, and was clearly trying to work out the geometry of the upcoming fight.

Thankfully for Rear Admiral DuBose, Vice Admiral Lee is not a harsh man, Orrick thought. *Although I'm sure he's going to have some words with DuBose, if we all make it out of this, about splitting the screen up three ways to chase some Japanese CL and a few destroyers that were apparently busy picking up survivors.*

"Sir, Rear Admiral Whiting reports the *Santa Fe* has been hit by three torpedoes!"

"What?!" Lee asked, his voice incredulous. "Confirm that report!"

Harsh man or no, it would appear that the Japanese are very lucky today, Orrick thought as the color drained from Jeter's face. *Fucking Long Lances, and it sounds like Rear Admiral DuBose might not be around to explain himself.*

Japanese torpedoes had been the bane of the USN's existence during the naval battles around Guadalcanal and the rest of the Solomons. Orrick still had trouble believing the reports from the men who had examined the specimens captured during that campaign. But regardless of whether those reports were true, either the Japanese cruiser fleeing east or her accompanying destroyers had just pulled off the equivalent of a Hail Mary pass.

*There's no way that Japanese light cruiser was aiming at the **Santa Fe** while running for her life*, Orrick thought, studying the map in astonishment. *There's 20,000 yards separating them and she'd have had to launch her torpedoes twelve minutes ago.*

"Sir, it's confirmed," Jeter said, having moved to where

the initial report came from. "*Santa Fe* is dead in the water and listing to starboard."

Orrick's eyes narrowed as he looked at the map and tried to consider the geometry of where everyone must have been when those torpedoes were fired.

Hell, if what they say about those torps is true, we're in range right now, Orrick thought, shaking his head. *There's no they'd hit us with anything other than a lucky shot, but the Japanese seem to be hitting all the jackpots today.*

"Sir, we're possibly in that torpedo fan if that Japanese light cruiser launched twenty minutes ago," Orrick said after a moment. "It's a long…"

"That's fucking absurd," Jeter cut him off abruptly from behind Vice Admiral Lee. Realizing he was holding a sound powered phone in his hand, Jeter hung up the device, looking at the map. "There's no torpedo in the world that can make 40,000 yards."

"I beg to differ," Orrick said. "I'm sure that Rear Admiral Wright…"

"Doesn't change anything we're doing," Lee snapped, putting a quick end to the burgeoning argument. Jeter glared at Orrick as he again picked up the.

"Sir, the *Santa Fe* is sinking," a talker reported somberly. "Rear Admiral Whiting reports per Rear Admiral DuBose signal, he is continuing to head towards our force."

Jesus Christ, Orrick though. *They've just decapitated the cruisers.*

"I'll worry about the damn Japanese torpedoes once we get their ships off the cruisers," Lee continued angrily. "Has anyone confirmed that large contact's identity?!"

"Sir, lookouts just confirmed it's the *Alaska*," Jeter said, stepping away from the phone that had a direct connection to the *Washington*'s bridge. "They also say it's starting to clear up topside."

Lee nodded at that news.

I'm shocked, Orrick thought. *The old man is one of the biggest proponents of blind fire in the fleet, yet he's actually held his fire. But then again, there's that plot, and he doesn't want to accidentally put a hole in a Seventh Fleet ship.*

"Bring us onto course oh eight zero true," Lee said after a few moments. "All ships may fire as they bear then."

"Aye aye, sir," Jeter stated, his tone jubilant as the talkers began relaying the information. Orrick could sense the *Washington* starting a rapid turn to port,

"Tell Rear Admiral Whiting we're changing the battle plan," Lee continued. "The *Alaska* will remain under his direct control. His orders are to keep the Japanese at a distance from us once their battle line has closed to visual range."

He's more worried about those approaching cruisers than he's letting on, Orrick thought. The *Alaska*, despite her powerful guns, had aways been intended as a "cruiser killer" rather than a vessel to sail in the battle line. Jeter had strenuously objected to the original plan of sending her forward with DuBose, so the compromise had been the large cruiser would fall in astern of the *Massachusetts*. However, with the *Santa Fe's* demise, Whiting was going to need all the guns he had to keep the Japanese vessels at a good distance from the American battle line.

Orrick turned and looked at the status board at the far end of the plot, which had been wheeled over as they started reaching gunnery range. A lieutenant commander stood beside the board, nodding as he listened to various radio transmissions. The radio net had gotten so chaotic that Lee had directed Jeter and the talkers to keep him abreast of the situation while he considered what needed to be done. Orrick watched as the young officer made two red hash marks through the *Santa Fe*, then used the same pen to mark three more circles on the *Wichita*. In contrast to the larger circle at the heavy cruiser's stern, the smaller symbols denoted cruiser fire.

Christ almighty, DuBose… no, wait it's Rear Admiral Whiting now who is taking a pounding, he thought grimly.

THE USN'S CRUISERS HAD INDEED "TAKING A POUNDING." However, in a validation of the USN's shipbuilding decisions and doctrine prior to the war's start, they were giving one in return. Unfortunately for Vice Admiral Kazutaka and his subordinates, the USN had made two investments when constructing the *Cleveland*-class vessels that comprised the majority of now Rear Admiral Whiting's command. First, they had used only the finest, densest steel available to build the light cruisers. Structurally, this made them more survivable than their larger assailants. Although the *Santa Fe* had blundered into DESRON 10's final Parthian shots and suffered underwater damage no cruiser was designed for, the Japanese cruisers had only managed to land six shells on the *Miami*, *Biloxi*, and *Vincennes*. None of these came close to damaging their target's maneuverability or speed.

The design decision about steel fed the efficacy of the USN's second decision, i.e., concentration on firing rate, accuracy, and ammunition to match the IJN's vessels. The combination of radar fire control and high-grade optics meant DuBose's light cruisers were able to fire almost as many shells with their aft turrets as the pursuing Japanese heavy cruisers had managed with their forward armament. Additionally, the combination of radar gunnery and superior optics meant that the higher rate of fire was also more effective. Thus as the light cruisers turned to mirror Vice

Admiral Lee's battleships' maneuvers and present their full broadsides, they found the range in devastating fashion.

The first Japanese heavy cruiser to suffer their erstwhile prey's wrath was the *Chikuma*. Designed as an "aviation cruiser," the *Chikuma* had launched the aircraft that provided the final weather report for the attack on Pearl Harbor. With her usual companions expected to serve as sacrifices to the north, the veteran cruiser was in the lead position closing with TF 34's screen. *Chikuma*'s gunnery officer, seeing the American light cruisers starting to execute a simultaneous "battle turn" to present their broadsides, had checked his own fire. It was to be his last earthly decision, as the first full broadside from the U.S.S *Miami* ripped the *Chikuma*'s director, bridge, and chart room to shreds. Barely forty-five seconds later, the next broadside put two American armor-piercing shells through the Japanese heavy cruiser's belt amidships.

The roaring steam pouring from *Chikuma*'s propulsion spaces hid the sounds of screaming, dying men from most of their surviving crewmates. Shouting to be heard above the din, *Chikuma*'s executive officer ordered the helm put hard over from the secondary command station. The heavy cruiser did not hav time to answer the helm when the only hit from *Miami*'s third broadside sent *Chikuma*'s XO to join his captain and gunnery officer in the afterlife. Slowing yet still answering her helm, the heavy cruiser responded to the *Miami*'s fire with a ragged broadside from the secondary director. Then once more the superior American ammunition proved its worth, as this time four shells knocked out the *Chikuma*'s No. 1 and No. 3 turrets, started a fire in her secondary flat and, most ominously, set the oxygen generator for the Long Lance torpedoes ablaze.

. . .

ORRICK HEARD THE *WASHINGTON*'S FIRING GONG RING FOR the second time and grasped the table in front of him. He saw Jeter speaking urgently into the telephone, then the compartment lurched with the shock of turrets 1 and 3 firing.

"Sir, Captain Wilkinson is repeating his request to launch a torpedo attack," Jeter said, clearly fighting to keep his voice even.

That's two requests in five minutes, Orrick thought. *There comes a point when you've got to give your commander time to think.*

"Denied," Lee said, with a slight arch to his tone. "As soon as they get over the surprise of seeing us, those Jap cruisers and destroyers are going to come right for us."

He's not wrong, Orrick thought as he looked over the developing plot. He had barely started doing math when the *Washington* gave a slight shudder.

"Stretcher party to the forecastle! Stretcher party to the forecastle!" the 1MC crackled.

That's not good, Orrick thought, loooking around the confined flag CIC. *Especially if we get a partial penetration.*

Once more the firing gong rang, and *Washington* shuddered. After another thirty seconds, the process was repeated.

Gunnery has the range it would appear, Orrick thought.

"We took a shell from one of their heavy cruisers," Jeter reported. "Hit one of the 20mm positions."

Lee acknowledged the report with a nod, continuing to look at the map.

"Gunnery reports we're straddling the lead Japanese battleship," Jeter continued a moment later. "It's one of those big new ones."

The *Washington* shifted under their feet, the vessel starting an unfamiliar motion.

Must be evasive maneuvers, Orrick thought.

"Okay, I need the TBS on the main speaker," Lee said. "Get a status report."

Jeter nodded, already barking orders. After a few moments, the loosely controlled chaos of TF 34's radio net filled the flag CIC.

Amazing how quickly the worm turns when big sisters get involved, Orrick mused, listening to DuBose's former subordinates talk back and forth. The *Santa Fe* had foundered, and the *New Orleans* was dead in the water. In return, it sounded like at least one, if not two, Japanese heavy cruisers were done for. The remainder, accompanied by the destroyers, were attempting to close with the *Washington* and the other battleships.

"That Jap commander's nailed his colors to the mast, sir," Jeter observed.

Is that a touch of nervousness? Orrick wondered. He saw the same things that had the Chief of Staff concerned, the Japanese cruisers and destroyers near fanatical charge being chief among them. As if on cue, the *Washington*'s secondary turrets began to join their larger brethren in engaging enemy forces. Orrick had been aboard the battleship during air attacks and had thought it almost impossible to hear inside the flag CIC then, but the cacophony that arose with the main battery now began to pound his ears.

The torpedoes! We have to remember the Japanese torpedoes far outrange ours. Orrick looked at the clock and was surprised to see barely ten minutes had passed since the *Washington* first opened fire.

"Sir, we might need to do a course change," Orrick shouted. "The torpedoes that passed…"

"*The **Alabama** has been hit!*" a talker screamed.

"*What?*" Lee cried. Before the man could answer, *Wash-*

ington shuddered hard enough that several men in the room were knocked off their feet.

"Fire in Turret 1! Damage control teams to Turret 1!"

The 1MC report caused Orrick's stomach to drop like a stone.

That sounds like we were hit by something severe.

"The *Alabama* has been hit by *what?!*" Lee bellowed again. "Goddammit, someone get me an accurate…"

"Torpedoes, sir," Jeter said, his face ashen as he glanced at Orrick. "The *Alabama* has been hit by three torpedoes."

"Torpedoes from *where?*" Lee asked, looking at the map.

Torpedoes from that damn Japanese light cruiser I tried to warn everyone about, Orrick thought, the churning in his stomach even worse.

"Bring us to course oh nine oh true!" Lee barked. "Now!"

ORRICK WAS ONLY PARTIALLY CORRECT. THE THREE torpedoes that slammed into the U.S.S. *Alabama*'s starboard side were not from the *Yahagi* specifically. The Type 93s had been launched by the destroyer *Yukikaze* at the pursuing U.S.S *Biloxi* shortly before the American light cruiser crippled her. With alert lookouts and conn officers who had been through the maelstrom of earlier surface actions, the *Biloxi* had adroitly side stepped the eight Long Lances then proceeded to finish the *Yukikaze* off in a hail of 6-inch fire. The eight weapons had proceeded on their date with naval history guided wholly by nothing but dumb luck.

As with the three weapons from *Ukikaze* that had struck the *Santa Fe*, the Type 93s merging with *Alabama* was sudden and wholly unexpected. Ironically, had the torpedoes merged with the American battleship at the same angle as those that had struck the *Santa Fe* the water pressure from *Alabama*'s massive hull moving at 28 knots would have prematurely detonated the warheads. Instead, by coming in from the large vessel's bow at a veritable "down the throat" angle, their warheads functioned exactly as designed. With the first weapon hitting at the junction of No. 1 and No. 2 engine room, the next barely 60 feet aft, then the final one in the No. 4 engine room, the "Lucky A" was all but disemboweled by over three thousand pounds of explosive in 45 seconds.

Water immediately began to flood into the three open spaces, pressed into the gashes at a massive rate as the *Alabama* slowed. Approaching rapidly from astern, the *Massachusetts*' bridge crew noted their sister ship's rapidly increasing list and put their own helm over hard to port. Before their horrified eyes, the *Alabama* continued to slowly rotate, her red lower hull starting to expose itself. Even as the vessel's damage control officer and his stalwart crew opened the valves to counterflood the portside void spaces, the Pacific sought to claim another victim.

"Sir, the *Massachusetts* reports that the *Alabama* is sinking," Jeter said grimly.

"Yes, I heard," Lee snapped. Orrick watched as the admiral gathered himself.

I'd be pissed too, he thought. *Suddenly this is not seeming like the battle we all envisioned.*

"Commit the destroyers," Lee ordered. "Maintain course north until we're out of this damn torpedo water."

"Aye aye, sir," Jeter said. He then began to issue orders, even as the *Washington*'s aft turret roared once more.

"Lieutenant Commander Orrick?" Lee said as the *Washington* started to heel over.

"Yes sir?"

Lee looked over at him, his expression grim.

"I'm sorry I didn't listen to you. Let's hope it doesn't cost us this damn battle."

IJNS Yamato
0825 Local

We are doomed, Ugaki thought as he looked out the *Yamato*'s flag bridge. *I do not know where those torpedoes came from, but they have lost this battle for us as surely as if they were fired at this vessel.*

The reason for his despondency was occurring roughly 8,000 yards away. Center Force's screening vessels had fought an incredibly savage, close range battle to get within 10,000 yards of the American battle line. Once there, they had fired over sixty torpedoes at their opposite numbers, the large American vessel that had apparently been harrying his force in the first place, and the four, now three American battleships that were heading north.

That last second turn will take them out of almost all of those torpedoes' reach, Ugaki thought. *I had believed those salvoes would kill at least two of them and cripple the other two.*

In exchange for their bravery, Ugaki counted a handful of his destroyers that remained. Of his cruisers, the *Chikuma* was drifting five miles astern, aflame from stem to stern. Ugaki had watched an American light cruiser riddle the heavy cruiser like a yakuza being gunned down by a Chicago gangster. That the same American cruiser had taken two torpedo hits and now lay on her beam ends was of little comfort. *Tone*, the *Chikuma*'s sister, had exploded from six hits from the large unknown American. *Kumano* had at least gotten her torpedoes away at the large enemy vessel before four hits had rendered her a powerless, drifting hulk.

The good news is she is not an **Iowa** *as we feared*, Ugaki thought, then laughed inwardly. *No, instead she is a wholly unknown capital ship class that is the manifestation of our folly in fighting the Americans in the first place.*

The eruption of three orange splashes around *Yamato*'s bow reminded him that he had a battle, such as it was, to fight.

Even running away that lead enemy battleship's accuracy is unholy, Ugaki thought, despondent. *She has hit us four times, although thankfully none of them of any real consequence. But we cannot let her open the range.*

"Sir, the *Kongo* reports she is losing speed!" Saito shouted.

The same cannot be said of the rest of the fleet, Ugaki fumed.

"Tell her captain he may maneuver independently," Ugaki shouted back, struggling to be heard over the crescendo of the *Yamato*'s secondaries and anti-aircraft guns. "Order the *Mutsu* and *Nagato* to continue concentrating on the enemy battleships, and the *Kongo* to destroy that damned enemy battlecruiser."

"*Hai!*" Saito responded. The younger officer was about to say something else when his eyes widened, his gaze focusing beyond Ugaki.

"Sir! The *Suzuya!*" Saito said, pointing.

Ugaki looked up to see the named heavy cruiser curving back towards the battle line, her bridge a mass of flames. The vessel was making over twenty knots, but was clearly out of control.

We do not have time for this! Ugaki wanted to shout. He briefly considered ordering *Yamato* to fire upon the closing cruiser, then stopped.

Fatigue is making me mad, he realized before doing some geometry in his head.

"All battleships, battle turn to port!" Ugaki shouted to Saito. "Go, tell them now!"

Saito looked stunned for a second, then nodded and disappeared once more toward the radio room.

I cannot turn away from the Americans, there is nowhere to run to the south, he thought. *At least turning north we may stay in visual range.*

Ugaki braced himself as the *Yamato* began to heel over to starboard. Watching, he saw the massive battleship's bow began to swing to his left. As she turned, the *Yamato*'s secondaries began firing even more rapidly. Ugaki brought up his glasses and swallowed hard as he saw the reason for the intensified gunfire.

There are over a dozen enemy destroyers steering at us, he thought. *And I just turned the fleet right towards them.*

Vice Admiral Ugaki's despair would have been far greater had he the sensors and time available for an accurate count. From the *Yamato*'s port quarter, shrouded in the smoke and destruction of a half dozen vessel's death throes, were the three surviving vessels of Destroyer Division (DESDIV) 99. Forced to ignore the thrashing, screaming survivors from the sunk *Santa Fe* and dodging the capsizing *New Orleans*, the *Clarence K. Bronson*, *Dortch*, and *Healy* stalked the Japanese battle line from just under 8,000 yards and closing. Just a bit further off *Yamato*'s port bow, the four DDs of DESDIV 100 charged forward from where they had been released from their escort of the *Alaska*. Finally, from 12,000 yards off the starboard bow, the four relatively fresh destroyers of DESDIV 104 were bearing down on the Japanese battleline through the Center Force's shattered screen.

Despite only having five of their escorts being in any shape to prevent the American charge, the Center Force was hardly helpless even considering the short range and Ugaki's tactical blunder. Three of the Japanese battleships had been designed in an era when a torpedo attack by small craft had been the proverbial monster under the bed for naval architects, while *Yamato* mounted former cruiser turrets as her primarily secondary weapons. All four battleships, despite the laming hits suffered by *Kongo* and penetrative damage to both *Mutsu* and *Nagato*, still maintained their full secondary fire control. Even with fatigued crews, combined the vessels boasted over 70 six- and five-inch guns capable of firing eight rounds a minute. In the roughly two minutes it took for the American destroyers to conduct their long, straight run to firing position, the Center Force's battleships alone had discharged over one thousand rounds.

Of the eleven sister ships to the departed *Johnston* that participated in the attack, four of them suffered her same fate. The *Knapp* and the *Cogswell*, both of DESDIV 100, each stopped a 6-inch shell with 5-inch magazines, while DESDIV 99's *Bronson* received a similar hit in her anti-aircraft storage. All three vessel were converted to flaming, foundering wrecks in the blink of an eye, their torpedoes unlaunched. The *Healy*, swerving around the *Bronson*, managed to disgorge her ten fish just before suffering her sister's fate also courtesy of *Mutsu*'s secondary. In minutes, scores of men were instantly slain, trapped at their rapidly flooding posts, or flung into the ocean.

Although not as instantly fatal as magazine hits, the Japanese fire rendered four more destroyers unable to obtain a successful launch point. Two destroyers, the *Dortch* and DESDIV 104's *Hunt*, were hit in their engineering spaces. The resultant damage staggered the DDs, slowing them beyond their division mates. Similarly, damage to the bridges or torpedo directors of the *Tingey*, *Caperton*, and *Cotten* rendered the trio of destroyers' runs moot even as they reached their designated launch points.

Even with the casualties, eight American destroyers reached 6,000 yards, the range at which they could use the faster settings on their Mark XVs. With their massive targets wreathed in the smoke of their secondaries, Japanese fire still impacting around or onto their vessels, and green, orange, and blue waterspouts from the American battleships obscuring their view, each gunnery officer chose their prey. Muttering prayers, profanity and, in at least one case, offering up his mortal soul, four chose the massive *Yamato*, three the *Mutsu*, and one the *Nagato*.

Surprisingly, lamed *Kongo* did not attract a single destroyer's ire... which was all well and good as the *Alaska* once more found the range just as the USN destroyers turned away. The large cruiser's salvo was a tight grouping that hit the former battlecruiser amidships and aft with four shells. The 12-inch rounds once more validated the Bureau of Ordnance's design principles, passing through the Japanese vessel's belt with almost comical ease from 11,000 yards.

Kongo's journey had begun in far off England, almost exactly thirty-one years and hundreds of thousands of miles before. The quartet of shells ensured that her long and distinguished career would not continue past the Battle of Samar. Two of them opened her remaining boiler rooms to the sea while simultaneously cooking the men inside with a massive gout of steam. The remaining two concurrently started a blaze in the vessel's No. 2 engine room while rupturing the oil feed to the now scalding boilers just forward. Burning, with most of her engine crew cooked like lobsters in their metal compartments and no power to her guns, the *Kongo* coasted to a stop while starting to list to port.

IRONIC THAT THE AMERICANS NEVER DEVELOPED WAKELESS torpedoes, Ugaki thought. *I can watch my doom creeping inevitably towards me.*

Ugaki and every other person on the flag bridge flinched as a 5-inch shell exploded above them. The American destroyers' guns had absolutely zero chance of penetrating the *Yamato*'s massive hide. This had not stopped them from firing at the superstructure at a prodigious rate.

The carnage among the anti-aircraft crews must be horrific, Ugaki thought, watching the two groups of torpedoes heading towards *Yamato*. Just beyond the incoming weapons, he saw one of their launching vessels begin to burn as at least two secondary shells hit. There was a high pitched rumble that caused everyone on the flag bridge but Ugakio to dive onto the deck. With a sharp *whang!* that Ugaki recognized as metal on metal, the No. 1 turret's armored facing rejected one of the American battleship's shells. The shuddering under his feet and cries for damage control to report to various stations told him that at least one other shell had hit with major effects. The announcements drowned out the sound of the firing gong, and Ugaki's whole body felt as though it was punched by *Yamato*'s riposte.

When full consciousness and awareness returned, Ugaki realized three things. First, Ensign Saito was shaking him. Two, the *Yamato*'s bow was starting to come around, and he was in danger of losing his footing as she heeled to starboard away from the turn. Lastly, and most ominously,

the American torpedoes were far, far closer than they had
been on both bows. Before he could take assessment of
what was going on, he felt the *Yamato* shudder once…
twice… then three more times.

Wait, what is happening? Ugaki thought, seeing the fifteen
wakes still closing with the battleship's side. *Were there more
torpedoes?*

"Sir! Sir! You need to lie down!" Saito screamed, then
began following his own advice.

Wait, he's right, Ugaki thought. Torpedo hits were
known to knock men off their feet or, in severe cases, break
their legs. For a moment, Ugaki nearly followed the young
man's guidance…then opted to ignore it while bracing
himself.

Yamato *is a large vessel*, he thought. *And I cannot lose visibility of this battle.*

"The *Kongo*!" someone shouted as the *Yamato* continued
her turn towards the two torpedo spreads approaching
from port. Ugaki took his eyes off the approaching
weapons to see the Imperial Japanese Navy's senior battleship clearly *in extremis*, steam and smoke pouring from her
midsection. As he watched through a forest of waterspouts,
first four, then barely forty seconds later, another quintet of
shells riddled *Kongo*'s port side.

That damned enemy battlecruiser, Ugaki thought, bringing
up his binoculars. He could see the large American vessel
cruising all by herself, only now turning *towards* the
Japanese force in reaction to what Ugaki could only
fervently hope were…

Oh no, torp…

THE INITIAL SHUDDERS THAT UGAKI AND WHAT REMAINED
of his staff had felt had been the salvo of torpedoes

launched from the massive battleship's quarter. Coming in from astern, three of the five Mark XV had prematurely detonated in the massive wake the 68,000-ton vessel caused at twenty-six knots. One of the remaining weapons passed *Yamato*, cruised on for another sixty-five seconds then, almost out of range, found the out of control *Suzuya*. Yet another indignity heaped onto the vessel in a morning that had suddenly become full of them, the Mark XV proved to be the literal tipping point in the Japanese crew's fight against progressive flooding. With a disturbing rapidity and the groan of screeching metal, *Suzuya* began to roll over to her starboard beam while still making a respectable fifteen knots. The combination only served to open her many holes wider, and the heavy cruiser simply steamed under the azure Philippine Sea before most of her crew could react.

The few men aboard *Yamato* who happened to be staring in the heavy cruiser's direction had little time to digest the unfolding horror before it was their own vessel's turn. Although the word nimble would have never been applied to the leviathan, she had been designed to be quite maneuverable for a vessel her size. Furthermore, in the confusion and chaos, two of the destroyer gunnery officers had misjudged her speed. The overall effect was like a well-trained elephant trying to dodge a couple dozen spears hurled at less than ten paces: Dumb luck, hunter's skill, and pure physics dictated there would be hits.

In *Yamato*'s case, there were four strikes. Two struck forward in the vessel's long bow on the port side, outside of the torpedo protective system. Underwater damage and flooding of any kind was undesirable, and the inrush of water began to swiftly affect the vessel's trim as she took on several thousand tons of seawater. However, if the battleship's damage control officer could have chosen anywhere to be struck, it would have been where both Mark XVs impacted forward of frames 18 and 27.

The next two explosions, however, were not so fortuitous. Running deep and striking near the bottom of *Yamato*'s prodigious armored belt, the third Mark XV hit on the starboard side near the junction of boiler rooms 3 and 7. So deep was the warhead, its torpex blasting through the torpedo protection system appeared to onlookers as a dud. Aboard the battleship there was little doubt of the warhead's effectiveness, as the jolt knocked many of the battleship's black gang to the deck across her entire stern. Objectively a wound neither grievously deep nor incredibly large, it was still enough to send the Pacific pouring into both spaces at a rate prodigious enough to doom almost all the men inside.

Seconds later and dozens of feet further aft, the fourth Mark XV hit the *Yamato*'s outermost starboard propeller near where the shaft entered the vessel's hull. No matter how innovative, warship designers had never been able to sufficiently strengthen such a point against underwater damage. The *Yamato*, even with more protection than any of her contemporaries, was no exception. With a terrifying screech the prop briefly ground in a gash enlarging oval before snapping and spinning into the dark depths below. So violent was the shaking, No. 3 turret briefly refused to turn to continue tracking the distant *Washington*, with the subsequent shells falling far wide of their target.

Worse than the futile discharge, the onrush of water through the massive hole exacerbated the list already beginning from the boiler room damage. As the men within No. 3 turret began the reloading process for the 18-inch guns, they realized the shell hoists were beginning to have increased friction when raising the massive shells. This was swiftly followed by reports of water seeping into the lower magazine. With due diligence, the No. 3 turret captain reported this information to *Yamato*'s bridge.

I SHOULD HAVE LISTENED TO ENSIGN SAITO, UGAKI thought, blinking to clear his vision from the intense pain in his head. The whipsaw effect of the torpedo hits somewhere aft had been much worse high in *Yamato*'s superstructure. Ugaki ran his tongue experimentally around his teeth to make sure he had not left any on the deck still below his cheek.

"Sir! Sir! Are you all right?!" Saito shouted, once again grabbing Ugaki's shoulder.

*I should strike you for touching me a **second** time*, Ugaki thought. His brain felt like it had been shaken in a custard bowl, and his vision swam as he tried to sit up.

Was I knocked unconscious? he frantically wondered, then forced that thought from his head. *No, if I was knocked unconscious, I would not remember hearing the damage control instructions.* With a start, Ugaki realized that he was having to fight to keep from rolling to his side.

"We are listing," he stated, to no one in particular. "Why are we listing?"

The *Yamato*'s intercom answered that question almost as if they'd heard him ask it. He recognized Captain Morishita's voice, and what the man was saying made the nausea twisting his stomach even worse.

The internal communications switchboard must be destroyed, Ugaki thought. *But instructions to flood **all** of the port voids means this list is not going to stop.*

Once more there was the sound of an incoming barrage from the American battleships. The shudder that ran through the deck told Ugaki that his flagship had taken another hit, this somewhere distant aft. Bracing himself,

Ugaki stood up, adrenaline and sheer resolve allowing him to ignore the intense pain in both his ankles and knees.

"What…what is the status of the rest of the fleet?!" he struggled to shout at his staff.

"Sir, we do not know," one of the petty officers replied. "The ladder to the radio room has buckled."

"*What?!*" Ugaki roared, swaying as if he had consumed an entire bottle of sake. He turned to look around him, then instantly regretted it. Bracing himself on the chart table and holding his head, Ugaki took a deep breath to avoid vomiting.

"Sir, it happened after you fell," Ensign Saito said. "Right after Commander Ryuunosuke fell out of the compartment."

Ugaki turned to look at the junior officer, then at the front of the compartment where the American bomb had blown a large, jagged hole. There was a bright red smear on the port bulkhead, near the jagged hole that had been blown in the flag bridge's side by the previous day's air attack.

"The torpedo, sir," Saito said, his voice trembling. "Commander Ryuunosuke was leaning to see what the damage was from the first two torpedoes forward when the third one hit."

He died a samurai's death, Ugaki thought. For a moment he wrestled with doubt, but the bow deck forward erupting in a shower of splinters, flame, and smoke cleared that thought from his mind.

There were four splashes that time, Ugaki thought, surprised at his own detachment. *The Americans have turned back to broadside. We are also so much slower.*

Very dimly, even more so after *Yamato*'s forward turrets fired once more, Ugaki heard a distant, familiar sound.

Death, he thought. *Death is flying for us.*

. . .

Banjo White One
0845 Local

Pretty sure Dante wrote about this once, Aaron
thought, shaking his head at the carnage in front of him.
The small motion caused a corresponding movement in
the *Avanger* and elicited a concerned movement
behind him.

Indeed, I think we should be seeing at least a human wave of
sinners running across the water on the horizon any time now…

"It's fucking crazy, isn't it?" Commander Pickering said
from behind him, his awestruck tone matching Aaron's
feelings. Pickering had been a last second addition at the
direction of Rear Admiral Sprague. As Pickering had not
qualified in an *Avenger* for over three months, he could not
fly an aircraft himself. So Rear Admiral Sprague had found
the next best solution.

In some ways I wish I had an actual gunner back there, Aaron
thought. *In others, it's nice to have another officer who I can speak*
freely with, even if he nominally outranks me.

"Sir, that's one word for it," Aaron said. "Terrifying is
an…oh my God!"

To their left front, a Japanese battleship was heeling
over, its massive pagoda mast slapping into the ocean with
a terrible splash. Five or six thousand yards from the now
sinking hulk, a capital ship Aaron couldn't recognize put
one last reflexive broadside into her sinking Japanese counterpart. At the same time, the mystery vessel's secondaries
engaged a pair of crippled Japanese vessels with steady fire.
One of these vessels, in turn, suddenly and violently
exploded under the barrage.

That was a Japanese destroyer, Aaron thought. *She just went down with at least a hundred men*, Aaron thought. He tore his eyes away to focus on Banjo Leader.

I don't envy him trying ot pick a target in this mess, Aaaron thought. *Especially with only a half dozen torpedo bombers*. The *Natoma Bay* had put up six *Avengers*. That was the extent of Taffy Two's strike, as the flight deck of every other surviving escort carrier had been holed by the Japanese cruisers at extreme range. Taffy One had been unable to dispatch any additional aircraft, having stumbled across another Japanese submarine while under simultaneous air attack from more suicide bombers.

"Holy shit! There she…"

The blast wave nearly knocked the stick out of Aaron's hand. Whipping his hand back around, he was just in time to see a second, then a third violent explosion shroud the capsized Japanese battleship in smoke and fire. A section of the hull, so large Aaron's mind briefly tried to convince him it was an escort vessel, tumbled out of the obscuration before splashing down.

"Jesus," Pickering said as the two consecutive blast waves shook their aircraft.

"No disrespect, sir, but I think the Lamb of God is taking a smoke break," Aaron replied, his voice quivering. "There are at least a thousand, probably closer to two thousand, folks who are probably waiting to talk to him when this is all over."

"Those poor bastards," Pickering said.

"I hope they get the express train to hell," Aaron snapped in response. "Sir."

Pickering was silent as Aaron followed Banjo Leader into a gentle turn. The largest Japanese vessel was slowly turning, smoke pouring form her stern and low in the water. He watched as a broadside from what he assumed was Third Fleet's battle line impacted around the monster.

There were four orange splashes, all tightly bracketed, and three hits that Aaron could see.

"Is it just me, or has that big one corrected the list she had when we first arrived," Pickering asked.

"Not your imagination, sir," Aaron replied. "But she's definitely lower in the water."

"Banjo Three, Banjo Lead," Aaron's headphones crackled. "You're the only one who has done this today, what do you think?"

What? Aaron thought, startled at Lieutenant Commander Barnes' question. *That was a dummy run for me.* Then he realized the man had a point. No one else in their small group, not even Pickering, had made a live torpedo run on a Japanese warship.

Shit, he thought. *Well, guess even a fake run beats a no run.*

Aaron scanned the Japanese line beneath him. Both *Nagato*-class vessels were sheering out of line past their larger, slowing counterpart. Both had obvious damage, but lashed out towards the distant American battleships with near simultaneous broadsides as they began to accelerate. There was smoke flowing back from the lead *Nagato*-class battleship, and a visible fire in her pagoda superstructure. However, the rear one was trailing oil from her starboard side.

Probably make this a lot easier for someone if one of those two bitches ended up lamed, he thought. *But which one?*

As if the universe heard his inquiry and decided to help, the lead *Nagato* was suddenly surrounded by a forest of green waterspouts and hit on the stern. The vessel's bow, already starting towards starboard, continued in that direction. Aaron watched as she began to turn even more to starboard, as if tightening maneuver.

"She's signaling!" Pickering shouted. "There must be something wrong with her!"

Must be nice to see with spotting glasses, Aaron thought bitterly. He watched for a long minute, another salvo of battleship shells landing far away from the turning vessel. The second *Nagato* breaking off her turn and starting to come back to port sealed the decision.

"Might as well get the hurt *Nagato*," Aaron finally replied. "I don't think we'll do anything to that big monster over there and the cripple be an easier target."

"Roger," Barnes replied. "I'll take Red section to her port, you take White to her starboard."

"Roger," Aaron replied.

I'm getting déjà vu and I don't like it, he thought, chills running across his back as he recalled his morning run. The subsequent aerial ballet took four minutes. Pickering provided a running commentary on the *Nagato*-class battleship's condition as Aaron concentrated on flying. The damaged battleship had managed to come out of her turn and appeared to be steering with her engines. She'd fired two more partial broadsides, almost as if she was trying to find the range, and been straddled by two in return.

You know, I'm suddenly glad I'm coming in from the opposite side of our battleships, Aaron thought. *Be a shame to come all this way and get killed by one of our own shorts.*

"Banjo Lead, I'm in position," Aaron radioed. "White section, let's go in and get some hits."

"Torpedo depth set to twenty feet," Pickering called from behind him.

Whoops, forgot that part of the drill, Aaron thought. *Yeah, I've done this before. Let's have me pick out the target.*

Aaron brought his goggles over his eyes, put the nose down, and started to descend.

One thing about jumping a battlewagon all by her lonesome, Aaron thought as the first tracers began to float lazily out towards his *Avenger. There's a whole helluva lot less anti-aircraft fire.*

"Someone's worked over her deck and superstructure really good," Pickering noted over the intercom. There was a rustle as the man's binocular straps went over his microphone. "Most of the open anti-aircraft guns look like the crews are dead."

PICKERING'S ASSESSMENT WAS PARTIALLY CORRECT. THE *Mutsu* had the misfortune attracting two American light cruisers' attention before Vice Admiral Lee had ordered his screen to finish off their IJN counterparts. As with their destroyer counterparts, the *Miami* and *Vincennes*'s shells had precisely zero chance of penetrating the Japanese battleship's armored belt or turrets. Their six-inch guns, however, would have been considered "heavy" artillery by any army in the world. When directed against the *Mutsu*'s upperworks, especially once the *Miami* had switched to high-explosive, their four minutes of work had turned the main director, most of the 25mm anti-aircraft guns, and most other exposed positions into a slaughterhouse. Indeed, *Mutsu* only remained properly conned due to her master, Captain Shirozu, and his stubborn insistence on fighting the battleship from the conning tower rather than the open bridge.

With her rudder cables cut by the *Massachusetts*'s shells and water leaking into both aft engine rooms, *Mutsu*'s options versus the six *Avengers* were somewhat limited. In the end, Big Mamie narrowed these decisions even further by hitting with four more of her massive 16-inch shells. Striking at the most inopportune time possible, the barrage ignited a fire in the bunkerage, eliminated the *Mutsu*'s plotting room, smashed through the face of No. 2 turret, plus severed communications between the bridge and engine rooms via smashing the central switchboard. Captain Shirozu would spend five minutes almost completely blinded by the secondary explosions and fire in his No. 2 turret while screaming useless orders that went little further than his conning tower.

MAYBE WE NEED TO CHOOSE A DIFFERENT TARGET, AARON thought, seeing the Japanese battleship starting to burn in front of him. *She's not even maneuvering now, and that second bow turret is done for.*

The rumble of secondary battery shells going past his head pushed that hypothesis right out of Aaron's head. A moment later the two stern turrets firing just reinforced how combat ready the *Nagato*-class battleship remained.

Nope, plenty of fight left, and we're almost there, he thought. Glancing down only briefly, he opened the bomb bay doors. Tracers flew all around the *Avenger*, but so far whomever was manning the guns was doing a very poor job of applying proper lead. The *Nagato*'s secondaries rippled again, a line of waterspouts appearing barely thirty yards ahead of the three closing *Avengers*.

"We're getting close to minimum range," Pickering shouted.

"Hold on…" Aaron replied.

"Shit! White Two is going in!" Pickering reported, his voice more disgusted than angry.

Just a little bit more.

The battleship was a harrowing long line of dark steel in front of him. Aaron could make out men running on her deck, looking like small ants.

Now!

The *Avenger* leaped up from the reduced weight as he

dropped their tin fish. Skidding the nose, Aaron tried to minimize exposing their belly to the battleship as he aimed to pass astern. From the corner of his eye, he saw one of Red section's aircraft opt to pass directly over the battleship. To Aaron's shock, the other *Avenger* made it seconds before the main battery fired once more, smoke and blast passing through where the *Avenger* had been.

Don't play poker with **that** *man*, he thought, keeping the throttle firewalled. The *Avenger* shook from a nearby explosion, shrapnel rattling off the side of the fuselage.

"Red section's fish are hot, straight, and normal!" Pickering shouted.

We might hurt this bitch yet, Aaron though.

FIVE *AVENGERS* HAD LAUNCHED ON THE DAMAGED *MUTSU*. The three on her port engaged side had misjudged her speed, distracted by the sound and fury of the *Massachusetts'* incoming fire. As a result, despite good drops, they scored only one hit. Still, the single aerial torpedo found the section of the *Mutsu*'s hull that had already been severely damaged by a destroyer torpedo. Passing through the warped and opened torpedo bulge, the weapon thundered into the bottom of the armored belt just below the No. 3 turret. Hot spall and fragments entered the *Mutsu*'s lower handling room, finding receptive homes in several black powder bags. Although not quite enough hit to cause a massive secondary explosion, a partial conflagration quickly sent a couple dozen men to their ancestors.

That fire was just catching hold when White section's two weapons hit, so close in time and space that they were perceived as one impact by those crew members in the vicinity. Not instantly fatal, the combined twelve hundred pounds of torpex overwhelmed the older battleship's underwater protection. Staggered, the *Mutsu* began to drastically slow as water poured into her forward engineering spaces.

"Three hits! At least three hits!" Pickering shouted, nearly deafening Aaron.

Wow, Aaron thought. *We really did it!*

"Okay, let's get the hell out of here," Aaron replied.

"How much fuel do we have?" Pickering asked.

You've got to be kidding me, Aaron thought.

"Sir?" he asked, trying to make his displeasure known without crossing the line into overt insubordination.

"Rear Admiral Sprague is going to want a report on how the action is going," Pickering replied. The man paused. "Plus you want to get back to the carrier just in time to be onboard when some of those suicide bombers arrive?"

I was actually planning on going to Tacloban and sitting the rest of this battle out, Aaron thought angrily. *But he brings up a good point.*

"If the *Natoma Bay*'s deck ends up holed, we'll have to divert to Tacloban," Aaron replied neutrally. "Rear Admiral Sprague will have a helluva time getting a report then."

Aaron could almost hear the gears turning in Pickering's head.

"If the *Natoma Bay* ends up holed, Rear Admiral Sprague will have a whole lot more to worry about than how the battleships are doing," Pickering stated.

Or like the other Rear Admiral Sprague, he might have nothing left to worry about ever again.

"Roger, taking us up to a good vantage point," Aaron said, pulling back on the stick.

By the time he got the *Avenger* up to 5,000 feet and turned around, Aaron wondered if they might as well have headed home. The *Nagato*-class they had dropped on had come to a stop and was now on fire across her entire aft section. The other *Nagato*, although still moving at around fifteen knots, was not firing anything other than secondary weapons.

"Jesus," Pickering whistled. "All four of that other *Nagato*'s turrets are knocked out. Surprised she's still moving, there's so much damage forward. I wonder…"

Aaron saw the flash of fire out of the corner of his eye and turned to see the American battleships were closing on both *Nagato*'s. Turning his eyes further east, he saw the massive Japanese super battleship had come to a complete stop, fires wreathing her upper decks, turrets akimbo. The damaged vessel was being peppered by several American small ships and the large cruiser that had seen off a *Kongo*. There was little or no return fire.

"Trapped like wounded tigers in a cage," Pickering said, his voice somber.

"They can surrender anytime," Aaron snarled, thinking of the burning *White Plains* earlier that morning.

"Unlikely," Pickering replied. "Their honor code will not allow it."

"Then their code is stupid," Aaron replied simply. "There's no point in killing all those sailor aboard their ships over some dumb adherence to whatever cause. Better to strike the flags and scuttle."

"Not very John Paul Jones of you, Lieutenant," Pickering chided. Aaron could tell the man's heart wasn't in the rebuke. Bringing them back around in an orbit, he saw the more distant *Nagato*-class's forward turret fly off and land bodily in the water. Additional hits ran the battleship's lengths, as a single blue then a single orange splash indicated two different American battleships had taken the vessel under fire. On the horizon, Aaron could pick out the dark, looming shapes.

"Can't be at more than 10,000 yards, right?" he observed, shaken.

"If that," Pickering replied, the trailing *Nagato* suddenly alive with hits as well. Roughly a minute later, the process was repeated, and the forward *Nagato* coasted completely to a stop with secondary hits starting to flash all along her length. The rate of impact on those were far faster, roughly a dozen a minute.

"It's an execution at this point," Pickering said quietly. "Murder, plain and simple."

Aaron felt sick to his stomach watching the spectacle. It did not take long, however. Suffering one last indignity of shells hitting her port side, the lead *Nagato* gave a visible shudder as if something finally gave internally. Corkscrewing to port, the massive pagoda mast causing her to want to tip even faster, the lead vessel's stern slipped quickly under the water. In a rush, the bow began to lift in the sky. Aaron noted the handful of massive, jagged holes that were too small for torpedo impacts.

They're going to call this Ironbottom Gulf by the end of today, Aaron thought. *Ye gods.*

"Big bitch is going too," their gunner shouted from below. Aaron and Pickering both turned in time to see the large Japanese battleship settle rapidly by the bow on an even keel. Descending like an oversized submarine, the big vessel seemed to just fall out from under her own central mast.

My God, how many years and millions of dollars have we watched die today? Aaron thought. *How terrible a waste have we suffered, and for what?*

He forced the melancholy thoughts from his mind, clenching his teeth in anger.

Fuck them, he seethed. *They wanted this war, they got it. I don't care if every one of those fuckers drowns. Hell, I'd like to help them.*

"I think we've seen enough," Pickering said. "Let's get out of here."

I've got a full run of ammo, Aaron mused, his heart starting to race as his vision clouded. *No one would care if I just ignored Pickering and went down there to get back some of our own.*

Aaron banked the *Avenger*, looking over the side at the struggling mass of humanity that was all that was left of two Japanese battleships. He thought briefly about his friends, his shipmates, the men who had been alive just the previous evening. Then he thought of poor Rizzo, entombed in another *Avenger*.

These assholes, if the black shoes have their shit together, will get to go to some nice island camp, Aaron continued to rage. *Then someday, they'll get to go home and fuck some nice geisha bitch, make babies, and talk about that time their fleet shot up some helpless American carriers.*

"Lieutenant Mackenzie," Pickering said, his tone concerned.

Meanwhile Rizzo is fucking…

"LIEUTENANT MACKENZIE!"

Aaron realized, with a start, that the Pacific was much, much too close to the descending *Avenger*. He brought the nose up, the pull up not as violent it could have been, so as not to stall. Thundering, the *Avenger* passed low over the group of Japanese sailors. For a brief moment, Aaron hoped to hear the chatter of the belly gun, but the torpedo bomber simply skimmed low over the struggling, oil clad men to the rumble of the Pratt and Whitney.

"If you're going to suicide dive into a bunch of Japanese, Lieutenant Mackenzie," Pickering said, his voice slightly shaken, "please let me out. I'd much rather jump out of an airplane and take my chances with those folks below."

Aaron laughed, the sound concerning even him as he let it out. After a couple of minutes, it turned into deep, wracking sobs as he brought the *Avenger* up and around.

NELSON IN THE LAND OF DEWEY

USS WASHINGTON
0600 LOCAL
26 OCTOBER 1944

"YOU KNOW, I'd have gone intelligence if I'd known it would get me back to Hawaii faster," Commander Jeter observed, briefly glancing at Orrick before running a straight razor across his face.

"Perhaps you should take it up with the man ordering me back, sir," Orrick replied, his tone somewhat pointed. He finished wiping his own face and folded his razor. "Especially as it seems like the kind of thing a Chief of Staff should do."

Jeter, the man who had made that decision, shook his head.

"I have," Jeter said with a grin. "He's a wise fellow. Realizes if said chief of staff goes anywhere near Pearl Harbor, there's a communications officer who might get the shit beat out of him. I wouldn't do well locked up in Leavenworth."

"You wouldn't like Kansas, sir," Orrick replied. "Cold as hell there and everything is flat."

Jeter cocked an eyebrow at Orrick in the mirror before giving him a mischievous smile.

"Surely not everything," he said, turning back to frowning at the realization he'd missed a spot on his chin. "I know a former Miss Kansas."

Orrick rolled his eyes.

"Sir, I'm from Missouri. Clearly that young lady was imported from my fair state if she had any curves at all."

Jeter just shook his head, chuckling.

"Well it didn't work out with the former Miss Kansas, anyway. And thankfully I met my wife a few months later. Keeps me from being involved in either state's border madness."

"Lieutenant Commander Orrick?" a voice called from outside the head.

"Yes?" Orrick asked, turning towards the hatch as he finished tying his tie.

"We've got that Jap admiral over from the *Miami*," the voice stated. "He's down in the brig waiting for you. Has some Nip ensign with him who claims he can speak English."

Orrick pursed his lips.

"Looks like I'll have something to tell the old man after all," he said, referring back to Vice Admiral Lee. "And Jesus, the *Miami*'s captain is a quick man."

"Yes, yes he is," Jeter replied as the messenger retreated back out of the head. "Although I don't think anything you tell the old man is going to change the report he's typing up for you."

"Hope he got some rest," Orrick said. "It was a rough day for him yesterday."

"Rough day for all of us," Jeter replied grimly, packing up his shaving kit. "They're still cleaning out No. 1 turret."

Orrick winced. He'd seen the structure right after the fire was put out, and *Washington* was lucky the anti-flash hatches had done their job. There was little doubt the battleship, along with the *South Dakota*, would be joining him in Hawaii by way of Ulithi Atoll and a stopover with the repair ship *Vestal*.

Good news is there's nothing else for that turret to shoot at, he thought. *At least, no heavy ships*. Vice Admiral Halsey, convinced that Vice Admiral Lee would have matters well in hand, had ruthlessly pursued the Japanese carriers and their escorts. The initial reports had detailed how the *New Jersey* and *Iowa* cornered the two Japanese hybrids and some cruisers around midday. Whether fleeing in an unexpected direction or trying to sneak south to conduct a surface attack, the handful of ships had been gunned down without inflicting even a single casualty on the American vessels. Making things even bloodier for the IJN, TF 38's combined airpower had been able to conduct multiple strikes against the fleet of apparently empty carriers. To call the resultant action a bloodbath was to render it a dignity that was wholly undeserved. Rumor had it that a single destroyer had managed to somehow escape, but Orrick did not think she'd get far.

Terrible thing about being on a small ship is they have small fuel tanks, he thought. *I think Vice Admiral Halsey did the right thing in stopping to pick up Japanese survivors. Surprising though given his feelings about our erstwhile opponents, but proper.*

"You'd better hurry up and get down there, Orrick," Jeter said, snapping Orrick out of his reverie.

"Yeah, guess I better get on that if I'm going to make Vice Admiral Halsey's schedule," he said. "Can't let that asshole Kinkaid get the first story out."

Jeter shook his head in disagreement.

"I don't think it will matter," he replied. "We just sank the entire Japanese Navy. What's going to be his counter to that? That he had his pants around his ankles as a distraction?"

Orrick chuckled as Jeter continued.

"The fact is, Vice Admiral Lee just became the greatest gun admiral since Nelson. The ghost of Dewey is up around Manila stomping his feet right now as no one will be talking about his fight anytime soon."

The two men stepped out into the busy passage, dodging a work party heading forward.

"Glad we didn't get close enough to board," Orrick observed as they reached the ladder leading down to the brig.

"Might as well have," Jeter replied somberly, looking back towards the bow. "I'm glad we have one of those shells as a dud. I don't think that big Japanese battleship had 16-inch guns."

Orrick shrugged.

"She's dead. That's all that matters."

"YOU SHOULD HAVE LET ME DROWN, ENSIGN SAITO," Ugaki murmured, pitching his voice low so their guard could not hear them. The young, large petty officer had already screamed at them three times to be silent.

We are in chains, Ugaki thought scornfully. *On a ship where there are literally thousands of men. Even if they had not taken my sword from me as a souvenir for their admiral, what devilry does this man think I possess?*

He allowed himself a small smile.

Moreover, if I had such devilry, why would I not have used it yesterday?

"Sir, the Navy had lost enough admirals before…"

The petty officer whirled towards them. Taking a night stick out of his belt, the burly man shoved the weapon in Saito's face.

"So help me God, if you say one…more…fucking… word, I will beat the living shit out of you," the man screamed.

"Which will be the last action you take before spending months on bread and water while we sail back to Hawaii," a stern voice said from the brig's hatchway. The petty officer whirled around, ready to continue yelling at whoever had spoken before immediately coming to attention.

"Sir, I…"

"I'm not interested," the newcomer stated as he stepped into view

A Lieutenant Commander, Ugaki thought. *Lovely. Guess I know who is here to interrogate me.*

"Ugaki-san, I apologize for the accommodations," the American rattled off in almost flawless Japanese, and Saito's face radiated the surprise that Ugaki himself felt. "However, I assure you, this swine will not be around to threaten you once I leave."

Ugaki watched as the petty officer looked on, confused that his superior was speaking Japanese.

"Leave us," the man said. "Send me your duty officer."

"Aye aye, sir," the petty officer said, coming to attention. The man quickly left the brig area, leaving the two Japanese officers staring at the lieutenant commander through their jail cell.

He must not know that I speak English. Then again, I am nowhere near as fluent in English as he apparently is in Japanese, Ugaki thought, studying the American officer as he fiddled in his pockets. Ugaki was shocked when the American produced a pack of cigarettes and held it over in their direction.

A peace offering, perhaps?

"I will, of course, have to light them for you," the American observed, apologetically. "While I am sure that my admiral will give me some leeway for my treatment, the captain may not be as understanding should you set your mattress on fire."

Ugaki cracked a bitter smile at that statement as he accepted the cigarette. After some hesitation, Saito did the same. The man produced a lighter, and Ugaki noticed with a start the Imperial Chrysanthemum symbol on the golden plated device's exterior.

"Where did you get your lighter, if I might ask?" Ugaki inquired. "It is very distinct."

"From a man I believe you knew quite well," the American replied, flicking the wheel. "One Isoroku Yamamoto. My father won it off him in a poker game at Harvard, actually."

Ugaki could not stop the hearty laugh that escaped.

"Your father attended Harvard with Admiral Yamamoto?"

"My father was a *janitor* at Harvard," the American replied, lighting Ugaki's cigarette with a brief fumbling that belied how seldom he actually smoked. "And a veritable card shark, from what my mother claimed. It's how my parents met, actually, as dad was collecting a debt from her boss."

"What does your father do now?" Ugaki asked, genuinely curious.

The American shrugged.

"Whatever we do in the great beyond. He got killed dancing at a wedding."

Ensign Saito looked at the American, aghast, his freshly lit cigarette dangerously close to falling out of his mouth.

"I am sorry," Ugaki said solemnly, in haling deeply

"We all gotta go."

Ugaki watched as the man exhaled, then turned towards the opening hatchway. A young ensign strode through the opening, came to attention, then saluted. The lieutenant commander returned the gesture.

"Lieutenant Commander Orrick, I am Ensign Conroy," the redheaded officer stated. "Petty Officer John said that you wanted to see me?"

"Petty Officer John is not to set foot around these prisoners again," Orrick stated. "If he does so, I will see to it that you and him both share a cell until such time as this vessel docks at Pearl. Do you understand?"

The ensign paled.

"Yes, sir."

"Furthermore, you will personally see to it that these men have proper food, bedding, and are allowed to sleep without harassment," Orrick continued. "You will eat whatever they are served, you will drink whatever they drink. Is that clear?"

"Yes, sir," the ensign replied again, eyes fixed on the bulkhead behind Orrick.

"Ensign Conroy, do you like games of strategy?" Orrick asked.

Conroy's eyes flicked to Orrick, puzzled.

"Sir?"

"Chess, checkers, acey deucey?"

"Yes, sir," Conroy said, clearly befuddled.

"You will find Commander Jeter, one each, when you are off watch," Orrick continued. "I will tell him where to find a small box which has two games inside of it."

Orrick turned to look at Ugaki.

"Vice Admiral, do you still play regular games of *Igo?*" the senior American officer asked.

Perhaps this man knows more about me than I realized, Ugaki thought.

"Yes, yes I do," he replied in thick English. Conroy seemed surprised.

"Good," Orrick replied in that same language, then turned back to Conroy.

"You will play at least three games of *Igo* with the Vice Admiral every day you are in charge of his prisoner detail," Orrick stated. "You will tell me who wins."

"Sir, I have no idea what you are..." the ensign started.

"Ensign Saito will teach you," Orrick replied.

"Sir, I have not played *Igo* that often," Saito stuttered.

"Good, then you will be an easy match up for Ensign Conroy when he is first getting started," Orrick replied. "In turn, Ensign Conroy will teach you acey deucey, which is the second game in that box."

In other circumstances, Ugaki would have found the identical expressions of shock on Conroy and Saito's faces amusing.

"I'll explain more later," Orrick said. "For now, leave us and come back in thirty minutes. Please send a mess steward in with some tea bags and boiled water. Make sure you emphasize to the mess hall that I will be drinking as well. I'd hate for someone to try and poison us."

Conroy nodded stiffly at that last part.

He wants to disagree, Ugaki thought. *But I note he does not want to disagree so much that he is questioning the orders.*

Once Conroy left, Orrick turned back to the two men.

"I have approximately one hour before I must depart this vessel," Orrick said. "I would humbly request that you do not make me spend this time in a one-sided conversation. You are the highest ranking Japanese admiral we have captured alive in the war, and Vice Admiral Lee has some questions about what happened yesterday."

It is not the samurai way to aid the enemy, even in defeat, Ugaki scowled, his instincts screaming at him to spit his defiance at the arrogant American. Just before he hurled the first invective, something made him stop. Looking around at his accommodations, he considered the vessel he was on, the other warships that had picked his subordinates out of the water, and the fact he'd watched the entire Center Force shattered before his eyes.

This is pointless, he thought, thinking about the pain that made it near torture to remain standing. The realization staggered him. *Japan has lost. I knew this as soon the first battleship shells started to land around* **Yamato**.

"I…" he began, then looked at Saito. Stubbing out his cigarette, Ugaki decided it was time to *live* for Japan for once.

"*We* will answer your questions to the best of our ability."

THE SOUND OF RAPID FOOTFALLS STOPPED ORRICK MID-sentence. It had been a fruitful forty-five minutes, even if Vice Admiral Ugaki apparently smoked like a chimney.

Going to have to get another pack, Orrick thought as the footfalls ceased and Commander Jeter stood in the doorway.

"The old man must be a quicker typist than I realized," he greeted the Chief of Staff. He was about to make a further wisecrack when he read the Chief of Staff's expression.

Man not only looks like he's seen Old Scratch, Orrick thought, *but was quite surprised to find said individual was five foot nothing with curves, knew his name, and had come to seduce him right there in the church.*

"Lieutenant Commander Orrick, a word please," Jeter said after a moment of working his throat to get the words out.

"Of course," Orrick replied, standing. He turned and gave a short bow to Vice Admiral Ugaki, who returned the gesture. Stepping outside of the brig hatch, Orrick saw that two different sailors were both waiting to enter the brig.

"I wasn't quite done," Orrick said, watching both men step in. "Hitting them with kindness worked. I hope…"

"Vice Admiral Lee is dead," Jeter interrupted, his voice husky.

Orrick took a couple steps backwards. He suddenly felt faint, and stuck out his hand to lean against a nearby bulkhead.

"What?" he started. "How?"

"Surgeon thinks it was his heart," Jeter said, then audibly swallowed.

Orrick saw tears forming in the other man's eyes as the Chief of Staff continued.

"He looked like he just laid down his head to rest for a moment. No sign of a struggle, no sign of pain. Just had his head on the desk next to the typewriter."

"God fucking dammit," Orrick spat. "I think he would have preferred a sharpshooter's bullet to that."

Jeter looked at him for a second, then the cognition hit him.

"Yes, yes he would have," Jeter replied. "But at least, like Nelson, he knew we'd won."

Orrick's own eyes burned at that statement.

Yes, yes he did, Orrick thought. *A victory, steeply won.*

"The only people who know are Captain Riggs, Vice

Admiral Lee's steward, and Rear Admiral DuBose," Jeter continued. "I suspect that Rear Admiral DuBose will probably contact Vice Admiral Halsey in the next twenty minutes."

At which point it will be known worldwide, Orrick thought bitterly. *Third Fleet staff can't keep anything quiet.*

"I just hope they don't put that bastard Kinkaid in charge of us," Orrick said out loud. Jeter looked up, shaking his head.

"That's right, you didn't hear," Jeter muttered. "Vice Admiral Kinkaid is dead. Apparently he was having some confab with General MacArthur aboard the *Wasatch* last night. Japanese sub caught her with four torpedoes."

"Holy shit," Orrick replied.

Guess that's what happens when most of your destroyers get shot up.

"Yeah," Jeter said. "That's the news I sent the steward in with this morning."

Hope Vice Admiral Lee and Kinkaid don't catch the same ferry, Orrick thought.

"MacArthur is still missing," Jeter replied. "They got the I-boat though."

Orrick gave a harsh laugh.

"Yeah, I'm sure that will balance out the news back home."

Jeter shrugged.

"I hope that insufferable bastard is actually still alive and has had to swim all night," Jeter replied. "It'd be fitting given how much coming here instead of going to Formosa has cost the Navy."

"'I have returned...' indeed," Orrick said, mocking MacArthur as Jeter chuckled. The chief of staff looked towards the brig.

"Any revelations from our guest?"

"Man is nuttier than Aunt Betty's fruit cake," Orrick replied. "But his plan was sound."

"For degrees of sound," Jeter replied bitterly. "Lots of young men dead from both sides because he didn't have the sense to keep running after Halsey mauled him."

"Don't think he could have done that any more than you and I could step aside and let Japanese battleships shell California," Orrick stated. "In any case, *we won.*"

BROOKLYN, NY
1145 LOCAL
26 OCTOBER 1945

THAT YOUNG MAN HAS A SET OF LUNGS ON HIM, LIEUTENANT Com...no, *Mister* Mackenzie thought as he stepped out of the taxi. A paperboy was doing his best to sell the diminishing stack of papers beside him at the subway station.

"MacArthur to lie in state in Manila!" the young man was shouting. "Secretary of War Stimson to travel to the Philippines."

"You know, they probably should have just quietly buried him at sea," Morgan said, stepping out of the vehicle's other side. "After a year in that water, I'm surprised there was anything left."

I wish I didn't know the details of how they found that bastard, Aaron thought.

The "Savior of the Philippines" had apparently been returning from visiting the head with several members of his staff when the *Wasatch* had been hit. Whether through dumb luck or quick thinking, the compartment's hatches had been shut.

Six days in that darkened space, Aaron thought. *Or at least, that's how many days were marked on the overhead.* The *Wasatch* had gone down in fairly shallow waters, but given the military situation, sixty-five feet might as well have been six thousand. They Navy had only decided to go get her code books and other material once the shooting had stopped.

"The man's getting a better funeral than Rizzo got," Aaron muttered. "Speaking of, which way are we walking?"

"Si…Aaron, you were never good at direction from a map," Morgan replied. "Always scared the shit out of us when we took off on a search mission."

Still takes a while getting used to being referred to as a normal human being rather than an officer.

"Yeah, well, I never got us fatally lost," Aaron replied. "Although there were times I wondered if that was about to happen."

Morgan looked momentarily wistful before the passage of an aircraft low over their head broke the moment of reverie.

"You got the invitation?" Aaron asked.

"Yeah, yeah, Aaron, I got the invitation," Morgan said. "Although I keep telling you, Mrs. Rizzo sounds like she ain't the type to turn anyone away. Even if she was, Betsy isn't."

Aaron looked over at Morgan and fought the urge to smirk.

I'm not sure of Morgan's relationship with the family, he thought. *I just know he's mentioned Betsy a lot since he picked me up this morning.* Betsy was apparently Rizzo's older sister, and friend of Gladys Hanigan, his late gunner's…pen pal.

"Shame you couldn't bring the wife with you," Morgan said.

"Well, with her mother in the hospital it's hard to find childcare," Aaron replied sheepishly. Morgan gave him a sly look.

"Maybe it'd be easier if you two could somehow stop making children?" the other man teased.

"You've met my wife," Aaron replied simply, smiling. "Witty, beautiful, charming…"

Morgan laughed.

"The way you talk about her is why you now have five kids," Morgan said. "Which I would not believe on seeing her. That is, until I met all of them."

I hope someday you find someone you love so much you just can't keep your hands off one another, Aaron thought, then sighed. *Even if I have no idea how I'm going to feed them selling insurance. Too many damn twins on her side of the family.*

Aaron looked out across the two rows of buildings off to their east. Just beyond the rooftops, he could see an aircraft carrier's island poking over the roofs as she made her way to the Navy Yard.

Then again, I probably wouldn't be able to feed them in that job either.

"Still amazes me we flew off something half that size," Morgan said.

"Or that we flew off something in the middle of the ocean at all," Aaron replied. "Still, given what happened to *her*, bigger doesn't mean better."

"What ship is that?" Morgan asked, nodding to the carrier. "I have to admit, I've flushed a lot of stuff like pennant numbers from my head in the last 3 months."

"Not useful in a steel mill?" Aaron asked, smiling.

"No, not particularly," Morgan replied. "Especially since I'm still learning the ropes."

"That's the *Franklin*," Aaron replied.

"Oh, the one that nearly sank off the Japanese coast!" Morgan exclaimed.

"Yes," Aaron replied. "Ensign Rhodes converted to the *Corsair* after Samar, got a quickie promotion. Was on CAP when the *Franklin* got hit. His flight lead got the bastard who dropped on her."

Aaron once again regarded the ship.

"Told me hearing the stories from his shipmates really brought home to him what being onboard the *Gambier Bay* was like when the Japanese were putting her under."

Morgan shook his head at that thought.

"I prefer to think it was just quick," the former gunner replied. "Like half those men on the *White Plains* probably never knew what hit them. That's what I want to think happened to all the folks we knew."

I'll let you have that little fiction in your head, Aaron thought. *Unfortunately, I got Rhodes drunk and got to hear the stories secondhand.*

"Where did he go after the *Franklin*?" Morgan asked, genuinely curious.

"The *Bunker Hill*," Aaron answered flatly.

"Jesus!"

"Same thing—was on CAP when it happened," Aaron continued. "Actually made ace that day, turned around, and his carrier's on fire."

Morgan shook his head.

"That's a lot."

Which is saying something, coming from either of us.

"It was," Aaron said. "Rhodes might have been embellishing somewhat, but apparently after *that* he was considered such a Jonah no squadron would take him."

Morgan looked at Aaron in surprise.

"You officers get weird about some shit," Morgan stated.

"First vessel shot out from under him, second vessel caught during flight operations, third vessel bumrushed by two *kamikazes*," Aaron recounted somberly. "I'm not surprised the powers that be let it be known he needed to be sent ashore on his next assignment."

The wind kicked up slightly, the fall chill causing Aaron to shiver.

"Which explains why he was an instructor out on the West Coast," Aaron continued. "I ran into him during demobilization."

"Well at least it worked out for him," Morgan stated.

"More or less," Aaron observed. The two men shared a knowing silence.

In some ways, no matter how horrible it might have been dying, a man's gotta wonder if what's next is better than living haunted by the ghosts of dead friends.

Rhodes had been well on his journey to the bottom of a bottle when Aaron saw him. A few discreet inquiries indicated that this was a nightly occurrence.

Several ways to commit suicide, Aaron thought grimly. *Some men just opt for installment plans.*

The vessel sounded its horn as if it knew the two men were watching, causing both to jump. That and the sound of distant bells chiming the half hour caused Aaron to glance at his watch.

"We better hurry up, it's still a few blocks."

"Oh, Betsy said that lunch will probably be ready late," Morgan said, shrugging as they started off again. "Her Mom isn't known for her punctuality."

Aaron looked sideways at his former gunner.

"You seem sweet on Rizzo's sister," he said.

Morgan colored slightly as Aaron continued.

"Even if her Mom is always late, she and other folks in her generation will be impressed if *you* are always on time. Shows reliability and respect for their time."

Morgan nodded, then gave a sly grin.

"I knew officer you was still in there somewhere," he said. Aaron shook his head.

"Maybe when I get to seven months out like you it'll go away."

"Right," Morgan said with a wry grin. "I'm shocked you walked away when given the chance, if I'm perfectly honest."

"Man has to know when it's time to walk away," Aaron replied.

"You won the Medal of Honor," Morgan said, gesturing at the blue, starred pocket handkerchief Aaron had stuffed in his suit jacket. "Guaranteed flag, that."

Yeah, well, flags are no good if you are dead, Aaron thought.

"Not a fan of the new jets," Aaron replied. "Things seem dangerous, but it's where the world is headed."

"Don't blame you, I guess," Morgan agreed as they turned the final corner before the Rizzo residence. "I'd have trouble trusting something without a prop as well."

A group of children were running around a blue house about halfway down the block. As they got closer, Aaron couldn't help but smile as he looked at the youngsters.

"Man, Rizzo wasn't lying when he said the boys in his family all look alike, was he?" Morgan said, shaking his head.

"I never had that conversation with him," Aaron replied. "But if he hadn't of said it, I'd still believe it."

Seeing the two strange men looking at them, two of the older boys stopped their rough housing to give Aaron and Morgan looks up and down. After a moment of looking at one another, then back at Aaron and Morgan, then at each other once again, the smaller of the two dark haired youngsters ran back towards the house's front door. The other one stood by the end of the walkway at the mailbox as the duo approached.

"You're with the Navy, aren't you?" the preteen said, his voice nervous.

Oh shit, he thinks we're here with bad news, Aaron realized. He put on his best gregarious uncle face.

"Very perceptive, young man," he began. "I *was* with the Navy…"

"*Kevin?!*" a young woman's voice came from the doorway. Aaron looked up to see a short, voluptuous brunette wearing what was obviously one of her best dresses come moving quickly out the door. Barging through the young folks like a destroyer on the hunt, she made a beeline for Morgan and threw her arms around him.

*Okay, so if he doesn't have feelings for **her**, she clearly has them for **him***, Aaron thought. From the way Morgan was hugging the young woman back, Aaron suspected the feelings were mutual. He looked up to see an older, taller version of the woman embracing Morgan just leaving the front door, followed in turn by an older version of Rizzo wearing an Army uniform with captain's bars.

Wait a second, I didn't know Rizzo had an older brother who was an Army captain, Aaron thought.

"Betsy Mae Rizzo, I *know* you were raised better than to make a spectacle in the middle of the street," the older woman said. From her tone, Aaron could tell her heart wasn't in the scolding, even as her daughter belatedly let Morgan out of her embrace. Aaron noted, however, that she did not let go of his gunner's hand.

"Good afternoon," Captain Rizzo stated. He started to extend his hand, then stopped. He looked as if he recognized Aaron, a fact that was confirmed as he came immediately to attention and saluted. Aaron returned the salute, seeing the confused look on Betsy and Mrs. Rizzo's faces.

"Please, I'm not in anymore," Aaron said sheepishly.

He then stopped, looking at the other man's chest. Without another word, he came to attention and saluted also.

"Sir, I mean, *Aaron*, do you two know each other?" Morgan asked.

"No," Aaron said, then nodded at Captain Rizzo's chest. "But I recognize that ribbon just as well."

Morgan did a double take, then looked at the two men.

"Just how do we end up with two Medal of Honor winners at the same luncheon?" he asked.

Aaron looked at Captain Rizzo, then extended his hand.

"Aaron," he stated.

"Patrick," the other man replied, then turned to Morgan. "Okinawa is how, unfortunately."

Aaron was astute enough to see the brief shadow that went over Mrs. Rizzo' face. For his part, Morgan winced.

Oh this woman has had some horrible nights, he thought. Belatedly he noticed the two blue stars and one gold in the front window. *Some very, very terrible nights.*

"Come on in," Betsy gushed. "Ma was just pulling the lasagna out of the oven."

"Gladys will be over in about ten minutes," Patrick said. "She had to run back to the hospital."

"Hospital?" Aaron asked.

"Yes," Patrick replied. "She's doing clinicals. But she can't wait to meet you, Aaron."

Betsy already had Morgan halfway up the walk towards the house, the duo trailed by several of the younger children. Aaron could hear the younger ones starting to ask Morgan all sorts of questions in the way elementary age kids did.

"Thank you," Patrick said lowly. Aaron looked up in surprise.

"I'm sorry, I don't know for what?"

"Gladys told me about the letters," Patrick said. "It was a rough time for her when Carson died. It helped to know he died a hero."

Aaron nodded somberly.

"I was glad to hear that he got the Silver Star," Aaron said. "I think it should have stayed the Navy Cross I submitted, but folks more senior than I felt like that was too high an award."

A cloud went over Patrick's face, and he actively shook it off.

"Well, I understand how that happens," the Army officer replied. "Trust me."

"Patrick, you and Mr. Mackenzie can talk shop some other time," Mrs. Rizzo chided from the doorway. "Get in here before the lasagna gets cold."

"Yes Ma," Patrick replied. His mother gave them both one last look before walking in and closing the door behind her.

"This Morgan, is he a good man?" Patrick asked quietly.

"If I had a daughter his age, I'd give my blessing immediately," Aaron said. "He's the one who made me swear to write Gladys."

Patrick nodded, and Aaron watched an array of emotions play over his face.

"Ma doesn't know it yet, but I've been dating Gladys for about four months," Patrick said. "She's a good woman, and I wish I'd known her better. But I'd gone off to join the Army back in '40."

Aaron looked at Patrick sideways.

"Battlefield commission," he said with a smile. "Anyway, I'm glad Morgan's a good man. I hope those two can work out the distance."

"Ohio's not that far away," Aaron said. "I'm just glad that *something* good came out of things."

Patrick smiled.

"We won the war," he replied. "Everything else is up to the folks back here to make it worth it."

With that, the other man opened the door. Aaron stepped into the living room and was surprised to see just how many people were there.

He's right, Aaron thought. *It's up to these folks to make it worth it. No use wondering any more about whether the cost was too high.*

ABOUT JAMES YOUNG

James Young is a science fiction and alternative history author and editor hailing from Missouri. Leaving small town life, James obtained a bachelor's in military history from the United States Military Academy then went on to spend six years as an armor and staff officer in Korea, the Pacific Northwest, and Germany.

After serving his commitment to the Republic, James returned to the Midwest to obtain his Masters and Doctorate in U.S. History from Kansas State. License for evil, er, Ph.D. in hand, Dr. Young now spends his spare time torturing characters, editing alternative history anthologies with far more famous authors like S.M. Stirling and David Weber (check out the Phases of Mars series), and admiring his wife's (Anita C. Young) award-winning artwork.

Website: https://vergassy.com/
Newsletter: http://eepurl.com/b9r8Xn

facebook.com/ColfaxDen
x.com/youngblai
amazon.com/James-Young

ALSO BY JAMES YOUNG

USURPER'S WAR SERIES

Acts of War

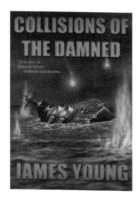

Collisions of the Damned

Against the Tide Imperial

USURPER'S WAR COLLECTION

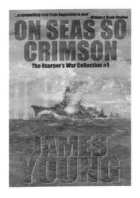

On Seas So Crimson

———

ALTERNATE HISTORY SHORT STORY COLLECTIONS

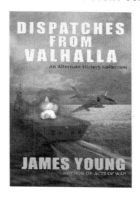

Dispatches from Valhalla

Coming in 2024

———

VERGASSY UNIVERSE

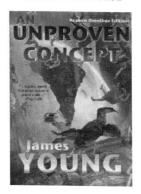

An Unproven Concept

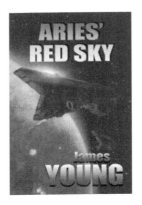

Aries' Red Sky

———

NONFICTION

Barren SEAD

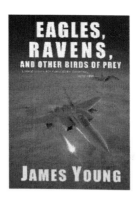

Eagles, Ravens, and Other Birds of Prey

Made in the USA
Columbia, SC
11 December 2024

49042300R00102